"Very well, Miss Smith." Ellis lifted himself from the chair.

She'd done it again. The man became an instant board around her. Straight, rigid, and totally unfeeling. "Why do you do that?"

"Do what?"

"Put up a wall of defense around me. Just when I think we are beginning to talk like normal people, you pull back into. . . into. . .a plank. Stiff, unbending, un—"

Fire ignited in Ellis's eyes. He closed them, and when he lifted his lids again his eyes were stone cold, dark, and piercing. "Good night, Miss Smith."

For a moment she thought she had reached him. But it was gone in a flash. With long strides to her door he made a hasty retreat. If the man had any appreciation for her as a woman, he sure kept it well hidden. No, she could never stay in Key West. Living under the same roof with a man she found so attractive she lost sleep over, yet who seemed almost repulsed by her, would be nerve-racking to say the least.

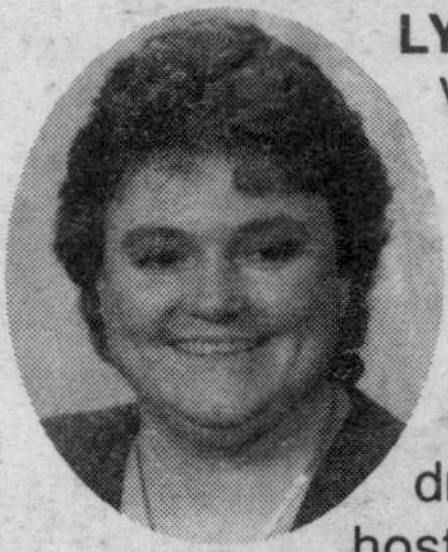

LYNN A. COLEMAN is a Martha's Vineyard native who now calls the tropics of Miami, Florida, home. She is a minister's wife who writes to the Lord's glory through the various means of articles, short stories, and a web site. She has three grown children and six grandchildren. She also hosts an inspirational romance writing workshop on the Internet, manages an inspirational romance web site, edits an inspirational romance electronic newsletter, and serves as president of the American Christian Romance Writers organization.

Books by Lynn A. Coleman

HEARTSONG PRESENTS
HP314—Sea Escape

Don't miss out on any of our super romances. Write to us at the following address for information on our newest releases and club information.

Heartsong Presents Readers' Service
PO Box 719
Uhrichsville, OH 44683

A Time to Embrace

Lynn A. Coleman

Heartsong Presents

I'd like to dedicate this book to my loving parents, Ron and Ellie Putnam. Without them I wouldn't be here, nor would I have had full use of their houseboat in Key West for my research. May I continue to be a sparkle of joy in your eyes.

All my love,
Lynn

A note from the author:
I love to hear from my readers! You may correspond with me by writing:

Lynn A. Coleman
Author Relations
PO Box 719
Uhrichsville, OH 44683
LynColeman@aol.com

ISBN 1-58660-023-0

A TIME TO EMBRACE

Scripture quotations, unless otherwise noted, are taken from the Authorized King James Version of the Bible.

Cover illustration by Lauraine Bush.

PRINTED IN THE U.S.A.

one

Key West, Florida, 1865

Bea scanned the approaching coastline. "Dear Lord," she exclaimed, her thoughts a jumble of fear and curiosity, "this is like heaven on earth." The crystal blue sea, the lush green palm trees, flowers bright and full of color in November—could this really be possible? So unlike the waters and shoreline of the New York harbor she had left a week earlier.

Yet she wanted to cling to Richard.

As her arm encircled the four-year-old boy's shoulders, the thought of parting with him tore at her heart. Poor, sweet Richard. Now that both of his parents were dead, it was her entrusted duty to bring him to Key West to live with his uncle. She grasped the ship's rail tighter. Ellis Southard had to be the most self-centered, uncaring man she had ever known. Not that she really knew him at all, but since he had received word of his brother's death, he had done nothing but upset her and Richard's world.

"Nanna, look!" Richard tugged at her skirt. "What are those birds?"

Bea turned to look in the direction that the child pointed. A huge bird, larger than any goose she had ever seen, bobbed up and down on the waves. Its long bill stretched down from its head and nestled in its chest. "I'm not certain, Richie. Perhaps we can ask your uncle Ellis when we see him."

If she could recognize his uncle Ellis. No pictures of Ellis were to be found in the Southard's home. From what she could recall from her conversations with Elizabeth, Ellis had left home to seek his fortune when he was a mere teenaged boy. Still, she hoped he would have some family resemblance, despite the fact that he was several years younger than his brother, Richard Southard II.

Bea donned her fingerless mitts, all the rage of new fashion, then nervously tapped at the ship's railing as she surveyed the crowd now gathering to meet the ship. The long dock reached far into the harbor. Effortlessly, the captain maneuvered the vessel up to the massive wooden structure. The seamen tossed heavy lines, and the pilings creaked under the strain of capturing the great vessel and bringing it to a standstill. As the boat lunged to a halt, Bea lost her footing and mentally chided herself for not remembering to use an onboard stance—feet slightly apart—to maintain her balance.

"Nanna, where's Uncle Ellis?"

"I'm certain he is here, Richard. Calm down, child, and let us wait for the captain's orders."

"Yes, ma'am."

Bea smiled and tousled the boy's golden blond locks. He looked like the mirror image of his mother—her dear friend. They had been neighbors, Elizabeth older by two years. But as teens, the age difference hadn't mattered. Nearly every day they spent some time together, even after Elizabeth married Richard.

He had been the man next door. Richard was twelve years older than Elizabeth, and thus never the boy next door.

Almost sensing her weakened condition would not improve, Elizabeth pleaded with Bea to come and live with her, to help care for the baby. So many years ago. So man changes.

"I love you, Richie."

"I love you, Nanna." He grabbed her by the hand and pulled her to the gangplank. "Come, let's find Uncle Ellis."

Bea's heart tightened. How could she ever give this child up? He was as much a part of her as life itself. Her father thought it time for her to marry and produce her own children. But Elizabeth had counted on her to nurture this child.

Young Richard, straining on her right hand, led her off the

ship and down the dock, casting imploring looks at strangers, yet too afraid to ask.

"Let's wait on the dock, Richie. Perhaps your uncle has been detained." A stunningly handsome man with reddish-brown hair and a trim beard nodded as he passed.

Perhaps father was right, she thought fleetingly. *Perhaps I should consider a husband and marriage.* Oh, she had some offers back home. However, with her responsibilities to young Richard, she never accepted any suitors. How could she possibly fall in love and simply toss the child aside? No, she couldn't do that.

Even the boy's mother, Elizabeth, had known she was asking a lot from Bea to give up her life, her own chance at the happiness of raising her own child. But they both agreed it was best for the baby. When it became clear that Elizabeth would lose her fight to stay alive, she assured Bea that, if Richard Sr. were to ever fall in love with her, she would have her blessing.

Bea smiled, remembering the day. Richard passed as a fairly handsome man, and perhaps she would have married him for the sake of little Richard, but she didn't fancy herself falling in love with him. He seemed too concerned with work, and he had little time for Elizabeth, though he did adore her in his own way. Bea couldn't imagine him having any time for her.

All that didn't matter. He was gone now, joined in heaven with his love, leaving Bea here with their child. Young Richard was now her responsibility. And his uncle obviously cared little for his welfare, or else he would have been here waiting for the ship. They had arrived on time. Perhaps she should just march back on the ship and leave, leave with Richard, and raise him herself. Her mind made up, Bea turned Richard toward the ship, marched briskly back down the weathered dock, and up the gangplank.

❧

Ellis visually scoured the decks of the *Justice,* unable to spot his nephew or the nanny. One thing he disliked most in people was lack of punctuality. He wondered if she had arrived at the New York harbor in time. He'd given her two weeks to pack and make her way to the city. "She certainly should have had enough time," he grumbled. He had noticed only one woman with her child on the docks. The child looked as if he could have been the right age, but his coloring seemed all wrong for a Southard. All Southards had various shades of brown hair, and only he had been blessed with blue-gray eyes. The rest of the family had brown eyes. *Always had, always would,* he reckoned.

Spying Captain Brighton by the cargo hold, he decided to inquire about two things. One, if he would be returning to New York or traveling to Cuba before returning. Two, if his nephew had actually made it on board.

"Good Morning, Jed."

Jed returned a hearty handshake. " 'Morning, Ellis. How's the sponge business?"

"Doing well. Are you heading back to New York?"

"After a trip to Cuba. Have some cargo?"

"Yes, but if you're returning from Cuba before going back to New York, I'll have more."

Jed rubbed his beard. "Wasn't planning on it; let me think a spell. I'll be picking up a healthy load of sugarcane."

"I'll take any available space you can give me."

"That's the thing about sponges, they take up room but not too much weight."

"Did my nephew make it onboard?"

"Handsome lad. Sure did. I saw him and his nanny on deck a few moments ago. They can't be too far."

"I must have missed them."

"They could have gone back to their cabin to get some of their bags."

"Must be it."

"This will be my last voyage for a while. The war's over. I'm tired, planning on settling down."

"Ah, a woman?" Ellis inquired.

"Hardly! The war took a toll on me. Privateering carries no honor, now that the war is over. During the war it was necessary. Now, well. . .now, folks just take you for a common thief."

"Sorry to hear it. I know you, Jed, you're an honorable man. Besides, I hate losing one of the fastest vessels to deliver my cargo."

"Aye, but perhaps a woman wouldn't be so bad either.

"Here comes your nephew and the prettiest nanny I've ever seen."

Ellis turned. The woman and fair-haired child. How. . .?

She was stunning—with lily-white complexion and hazel eyes. Worried eyes. Young eyes. Weren't nannies old and gray? Shouldn't they be?

❧

"Pardon me, Captain Brighton, but we seem to have a problem."

The captain stood with the handsome stranger she had noticed earlier. Perhaps she shouldn't interrupt, but she did want another glimpse at the gentleman with such strong shoulders and distinguished face. *What's wrong with noticing a striking man?* she rationalized.

"Miss Smith, may I introduce you to Mr. Ellis Southard."

Ellis Southard? She examined him closely. He had brown hair, but redder than she expected. Perhaps the tropical sun had painted it. His eyes, oh my, they were so like little Richard's eyes—the same blue-gray, same shape, though older, more mature. More passionate. Bea swallowed.

"Forgive me, Miss Smith, I assumed you were the child's mother." Ellis bent down on one knee before the boy. "You must be Richard?"

"Yes, sir. Are you my uncle Ellis?"

"That I am, Son, that I am."

Richard stepped out farther from behind Bea's skirt, but still clung to it. For all the child's excitement at meeting his uncle, he remained naturally afraid of a stranger. Why wouldn't he be? The poor child already had so much loss in his short life, and was now about to lose the only mother he'd known. Bea had hoped to stay on for a while to transition the child into a relationship with his uncle, but now uncertainty loomed. The man was too dangerously appealing.

Ellis extended a hand. Richard took it. "Tell me, Son, what do you think of this tropical isle?"

Richard's other hand trembled with fear on her skirt. Bea placed her hand on his back. "Richard, perhaps your uncle Ellis knows what kind of bird that is." She pointed to the one that had caught his attention earlier.

Ellis Southard followed her lead. "It's a pelican. Did you know those particular birds can swallow fish whole?"

"Pelican?" Richard answered.

"Yes, pelican. Their beaks have a floppy pouch they fill with fish and water. When the bird closes its beak, it spits out the water and swallows the fish."

Richard's eyes bulged as he strained to watch the interesting new bird.

"I've been unable to find a nanny for the child," Ellis said, standing again and meeting Bea's eyes. "Would you be willing to stay on for a week or so, Miss Smith?"

What an answer to prayer! On the other hand, her attraction to this man scared her. "It would be my privilege, Mr. Southard."

"Excellent. If you would excuse me, I need to take care of a bit of business. Then I'll bring you and the child to my home."

The child! *He can't even call Richard by his name?* Bea fumed. *Oh Lord, this man can't possibly be meant to care for Richie. He has the compassion of a gnat!*

Rather than speak her mind, she stepped back and led Richie to the railing of the ship where he kept a vigil on the exotic bird. She could see his mind working. She knew he hoped the bird would get hungry so he could watch it eat.

"Nanna, why can't you stay with me?"

"Because I live in New York." Of course, the idea of moving back into her family home after she'd been a nanny for four years bothered her tremendously. She loved her folks, but having tasted independence she didn't want to go back to the waiting season of balls and having men call on her. Well, perhaps gentlemen callers wouldn't be so bad, but. . .she wanted to do things on her own. Her folks talked about having another coming-out party on her behalf since she had been kept from social events for years.

"But why?" Richard interrupted her reverie.

Bea knelt down beside Richard and pulled him into her arms. "I will visit as often as I can, Richie. I love you as if you were my own. Your uncle Ellis is family; he will take good care of you."

She prayed she wasn't lying to him. She had serious questions about the man's parenting abilities, despite his brief attempts at friendliness toward Richie. Besides, what would a single man do with a child?

Perhaps he had married. She hadn't heard news from him prior to his letter concerning the house, the lands, and arrangements for her to bring Richard to him. She supposed it amounted, in part, to what bothered her the most about him. He hadn't come to New York to take care of family business himself. Instead he barked out his orders and dictated from Key West.

His brother had been no different, telling his ailing wife he was going off to war. Then he arranged for people to run the farm and left. Well, he had spent several private days with his wife before going. And he had come back as often as possible to oversee the house, look in on his son, and do whatever he could with his few days leave. But those times had been rare. Of course, he had come as soon as he had received word of Elizabeth's passing. Bea had even seen him weeping at her grave. He truly did love her, Bea believed. He just didn't see marriage as a partnership.

Bea's parents, on the other hand, worked hand-in-hand. True, Mother took care of most of the social activities.

Never-theless, Bea had often heard her parents discussing matters of investments together. She knew her father was a rare man. Not many took stock in a woman's opinion when it came to business. But her mother had a head for numbers. "God's special blessing," her father always said.

She kissed Richard's cheek. "Shh, my love, everything will be all right. God is watching over you and He loves you far more than I."

Richie hugged her hard and returned her kiss. Bea held back the tears burning the edge of her lids.

"Miss Smith, if you are through coddling the child, it is time to be on our way."

Bea stood up straight and eased the child down to the deck. *Oh Lord, please tell me this isn't a mistake. This man is insufferable.*

two

Ellis caught Jed's chastising glance and realized he had been abrupt, possibly even rude, with Miss Smith. Quickly coming to his own defense, he rationalized how women on Key West were rare commodities, and to know he was going to have a beautiful one in his house with a tender loving touch. . .he would definitely need to be on his guard.

She nodded in his direction, her lips tight, her jaw tense. *Yes sir, this woman will definitely need to be kept at a distance.* Even angry she looked appealing. With all the men on Key West, Miss Smith would surely have more invitations to social activities than he'd had for the past year. Ellis felt oddly uncomfortable with the prospect. It might be best to have the temptation of a pretty face gone. On the other hand, the idea of another man. . . Well, he just wouldn't allow himself to follow that particular line of thinking.

"I have a carriage to bring your baggage to the house," he said, trying to ease the tension.

"Uncle Ellis, do you have a boat?"

"Yes, a small one. Did you enjoy the sail from New York, Richard?"

"Yes, sir. I've never been on a sailboat before."

"May I suggest, on the evenings I'm able, we go for a sail and perhaps do some fishing."

"Can I, Nanna?"

"Of course, dear. Whatever your uncle Ellis would like. He's your parent now."

Richard knitted his brows. "My daddy died in the war."

"I know, Son." Ellis was still coming to terms with his brother's death. He was amazed at how well the child was handling the tragedy.

"Did you know my daddy?"

"We were brothers. I grew up with him." Ellis looked over to Miss Smith. What had she told the lad about him? She glanced away after acknowledging she had discussed him with the child.

"Nanna told me you were my daddy's brother. I don't have a brother."

"I know, Richard," Ellis replied.

"But Billy has a brother, and his brother lives with him. How come you didn't live with my daddy?"

Ellis reached for Richard's hand, then thought better of it. He was so timid a few minutes ago. He didn't want to spook the child. "That, Son, is a very long story. Let me take you to my home and get Miss Smith out of this hot sun."

Richard nodded.

"Mistress Smith, my carriage is this way." Ellis thought long and hard, trying to remember the woman's first name, but for the life of him he couldn't remember. He was not a man given to forgetfulness. This was indeed something else to ponder. She seemed as beguiling as some of the stories he'd heard of sea sirens in ancient mythology.

Her thick, dark dress would be far too exhausting in this region. He hoped she had brought her summer apparel, as he had requested, along with Richard's belongings. A simple wool coat for the coldest of days in the winter was all that was needed. He reckoned she didn't have a clue what November in the Florida straits would be like. At least her hat had a wide brim and would protect her fair skin from the hot rays of the sun.

❧

Bea followed Ellis Southard's lead. He seemed to talk with compassion to Richard, and he certainly gave him his full attention. She found this a surprising and welcome relief, compared to the way most adults generally ignored children.

The port was busy. Ships of all shapes and sizes lined the harbor. Few horses and carriages lined the streets, but activity flourished. She had tried to learn about this island, so new to the territory, but little was written. Richard Sr. had informed her of a troop of Union soldiers stationed on the island from the beginning of the Civil War, and she had seen the fort. He had wanted to be stationed here, in the hope of spending some time with his brother, but Richard had spent most of his time in Virginia and other areas of heavy fighting.

Bea wondered if Ellis was a Southern sympathizer. The war was over, but she knew so little of the man. Her mother had told her, on more than one occasion, political matters were for men and she'd best not get involved. For the most part she heeded her mother's admonition, but only due to the fact she was busy caring for a small child. At one point she had followed Elizabeth's instructions and buried the family silver in the yard. It had been passed down for several generations and no war, no matter what the issue, would take that away from the Southards. They, of course, had fed many of the troops as they worked their way south. Never had she felt her life, or little Richard's, was in danger, but it was a weary time. Reports of families being torn apart, brothers fighting against brothers, cousins against cousins—such an ugly mess.

However, Bea was convinced slavery was cruel and heartless. Now, as she looked around the island, she saw black men, white men, and Hispanics working side by side. Could this place truly be a paradise?

She fanned herself. The sun was high in the sky and she was suffocating. Why had she worn such a heavy dress today? The first several days at sea were cold. Very cold. But the last two days, the temperatures had been warming. Now, the intense heat of the bright afternoon sun against the perfect sky of blue made her thirsty and a bit weak.

She needed to get out of these warm clothes. "Pardon me, Mr. Southard. How far must we travel until we reach your home?"

"Not far at all. The island is quite small. You could walk to my home in a few minutes' time."

Walk? The idea worried her. "I thought you said you had a carriage?"

"I did, and I do. As soon as we arrive at my home I'll show you the guest house. You'll be staying in the cottage, and Richard will be staying with me in the main house."

The guest house? She wouldn't be sleeping next to Richard? What if he cried out for her in the middle of the night? Of course he hadn't done that for a long time, not since he was sick the last time, but still. . . .

"Miss Smith, I don't believe it is proper for a man to have a single woman in his home without staff who also live in the home."

"Oh." Bea blushed. He did have a point. But she was the child's nanny. Wasn't that considered staff?

"Since you're no longer the child's nanny, I think it improper."

Could he read her mind? Bea nodded and bit back her counter-argument. As far as she was concerned, she was more than a nanny to Richard. But he was right. Her time of releasing and letting the child go had come. "A time to embrace and a time to refrain from embracing," Ecclesiastes 3:5, came to mind. Wasn't that the Scripture the Lord had been working on her heart for months now? Bea let out a deep breath and stepped up into the carriage while Ellis stowed their baggage.

The carriage moved slowly from the docks. The variety of trees, flowers, and unfamiliar sights took Bea's mind off her present discomfort. Further in from the shore were more trees and a gentle breeze. Mixed with the shade, they eased her discomfort.

The house, a two-story wooden structure with shutters, stood proudly within a tropical garden. Fruit trees of every imaginable kind lined the yard. In the rear of the yard stood a cute cottage, looking to Bea for all the world as if a ship were buried in the earth from the deck down. The cottage gave the appearance of a ship's cabin, perhaps the captain's quarters.

Ellis jumped down and helped Bea to the ground. His firm hands on her waist as he guided her down the long step from the carriage gave her reason to catch his eyes, blue-gray, and as deep as the northern seas.

He released her the instant her feet were on the ground. Her sides ached for his touch. Bea shook her head slightly, fussing with herself to take a logical approach to all this. She suddenly felt faint from the heat. She'd been to sea for days, perhaps her equilibrium was off. The sight of a handsome face certainly couldn't account for it, especially since the man was so impersonal and seemed to care only for the harsh reality of profit-making.

"The guest cottage was a ship's cabin. The former owner of this property, Captain Curtis, salvaged it and turned it into this cottage."

"It's quite unique." The place really was charming, she had to admit. But she was still agitated over Ellis's comment at the boat about her coddling Richard. *Perhaps feminine words and gestures are not endearing to the gentleman,* she thought, fighting back the sarcasm.

"I trust you will find everything you need. Dinner is served at five—you'll join us for meals."

Was that an order? Bea fought down her defensive posture and thanked him.

He pointed out the outdoor water closet and other necessities for her comfort.

Richard pouted. "I want to stay with Nanna."

"Richie, your uncle Ellis has a room just for you in his big house." Bea stroked his blond hair and smiled.

"Son," Ellis knelt down beside the child. He'd done that before. Maybe he did have a heart of compassion for the lad. "If after seeing your new room you still wish to spend the night out here in the cottage, it will be all right. Miss Smith will be close by. In fact, you can look out your window and see her cottage."

"Really?" Richard's eyes implored his uncle's. Two pairs of similar eyes searched each other. Bea turned. She couldn't allow Richard to see her pain.

"Naturally. Shall I show you your new room so that Miss Smith can have some privacy and gain some comfort from this heat?"

Richard propelled himself from the cottage. *He has only just met his uncle,* Bea lamented silently, *and is already willing to leave me, even forgetting to say good-bye.* Tears edged her eyes. No, she wouldn't cry. Not now. Not yet. Later, perhaps. When no one would know.

❧

The memory of Miss Smith's delicate waist in his hands to aid her descent from his carriage had reinforced his decision to put her in the guest house. Face-to-face, day in, day out with a beautiful woman, together with the present shortage of women on the island, would press any sane mane to his limits. He couldn't fault little Richie for wanting to stay close to her. Who wouldn't?

He mounted the porch stairs of his newly acquired home two at a time. "Come on, Richard, let me show you to your brand-new room." Curious in Miss Smith's presence, he'd felt the need to be formal, dignified, quite the opposite of his normal boisterous self. He reached down and scooped Richard up, placing him on his shoulders. "So tell me, Son. Does your Nanna have a first name?"

"Nanna!"

Of course. Wasn't his own mother always "Mom"? Ellis chuckled. "I guess I should say, what do other people call Miss Smith?"

"Bea."

Bea. Beatrice. That's it! How could he have forgotten? After all, that was his maternal grandmother's name.

"So, do you like fishing, Richard?"

Ellis could feel the child nod against the back of his head and neck. "Here we are, Son, do you like it?" Together they surveyed the room's single oak-framed bed, an old sea captain's chest he had purchased for the child's toys, and a small chest of drawers he had acquired from a recent wrecking expedition. A small bamboo fishing pole leaned up against the chest of drawers, just the right size for a young boy. One of the things Ellis enjoyed about Key West was the variety of items that came to port. Wrecking, or rather ship salvaging, had been the island's primary income before the war, as ships from around the world ran aground off the various coral reefs.

He settled Richard down to the floor and watched as the lad soaked up his surroundings. His eyes focused on the fishing pole.

"For me?"

"For you. I thought perhaps we could go fishing together. Would you like that?"

Richard nodded his head and tentatively reached for the pole.

"Go ahead, pick it up." Ellis sat on the bed. "How does it feel in your hands?"

Richard worked his tongue between his teeth as he held the pole in his hands, his eyes wide with excitement. Ellis breathed a sigh of relief. He didn't know anything about raising kids, but figured he'd focus on things he had enjoyed doing when he was a boy.

His only problem would be caring for the child when he was at work. He had been prone to spend long days away from the house, sunup to sundown. With young Richard now depending on him, he would have to adjust his schedule. But he would need to work, and he would need a nanny to watch over the lad.

His mind raced back to the beautiful woman in his guest house. He hoped she was well. She had looked completely exhausted from the heat. He made a mental note to talk with Cook and have some lemonade taken over to her. She would need to drink a lot to become acclimated to this climate.

"Uncle Ellis? Can Nanna go fishing with us?"

"If she would like." He hadn't known many women from New York who liked to fish. Here in Key West it wasn't unusual, but someone from New York. . .well, he'd never seen it. "Have you been fishing before?"

Richard nodded his head. It seemed he didn't speak often. Ellis wondered if it was just shyness.

"Who took you fishing? Your daddy?"

"Nanna. Daddy was at war." Richard placed the pole back where he had found it.

She took the boy fishing? *Hmm, maybe she doesn't coddle the child after all.* "Did she teach you to bait a hook?"

"Nanna does that. She says it's hard to get the worm to stay on the hook."

Ellis grinned. The image of the fair-skinned, very proper young woman wrapping a worm on a hook intrigued him.

"Well, let me introduce you to Cook."

"Cook?"

"She's someone I hired to prepare meals and do some cleaning for me."

Richard knitted his eyebrows together. "Nanna cooks."

"Come on, I'll introduce you."

Ellis scooped the child into his arms and had him ride on his hip. A pleasing sense of comfort seemed to wrap the inside of his body even as little Richard's small frame wrapped the outside. He hoped and prayed it brought comfort to Richard as well.

"Good afternoon, Cook. How are you today?"

"Fine, Mr. Ellis. Would this be young Master Southard I've been hearin' about?"

"That's right. Richard, this is Cook. Cook, this is Richard, my nephew."

"Fine lookin' young lad. He has your eyes, Mr. Ellis. But his hair is much fairer than yours."

"My mommy had blond hair," Richard stated proudly. "Nanna says I have her hair."

"Nanna?" Cook inquired.

"Nanna is his term for his nanny. She's in the guest house. Would you be so kind as to run over and give her some of your fine lemonade?"

"No sir, but I'll give her some limeade."

Ellis chuckled. "Whatever you think best, Cook." He turned to Richard, still in his arms. "Richard, do you wish to explore the house or help me with your baggage?"

"Can I explore?"

"Sure can. I haven't explored it all yet. If you find anything of interest, let me know." Ellis watched the boy run out of the kitchen and down the hall.

Cook's broad smile disappeared from her dark, round face. "Now, why is the boy's nanny out all alone in the guest house?" she demanded, planting her strong hands on ample hips, her full figure going rigid.

"Because you won't move into my house. How's a man to keep up with proper etiquette if he has a single woman living with him?"

"Fiddlesticks, ain't no high society image here to maintain. What's the real reason? I fixed up the spare room, just like you asked."

three

Ellis shifted nervously. He'd never been able to keep Cook from prying. The woman was incredible. He couldn't imagine her children ever getting away with anything. "Once you meet her, you'll understand."

"Ah, so she struck your fancy."

Ellis blushed. A retreat was his only option, before she learned more than he had a mind to let her know. "Please, take her some limeade." He turned around and quickly made his exit. Two steps out of the room, he heard Cook chuckling under her breath.

❧

Inventory ledgers, exporting records—all needed posting. Ellis tried for the fifteenth time to concentrate on the books before him. He dabbed the pen in the inkwell one more time. He had planned the day off, giving himself and his nephew time to get acquainted. He hadn't planned on his nephew's nanny creating within him a driving force to flee back to work at the docks.

Maybe that isn't a bad idea, Ellis thought. He pushed back his chair and walked over to the window facing the small cottage. His hands clasped behind his back, he stood there, staring absentmindedly. A moment later Cook scurried toward the cottage with a tray and a pitcher of limeade. He watched as the door opened, but Miss Smith remained in the shadows as Cook entered the cottage. Disappointed, he turned around and faced the room.

Why was he disappointed?

Breaking his reverie, Richard's scream assaulted his ears. "Uncle Ellis!"

He bolted out of his office down the hall toward the

direction of the scream. His heart racing, blood pumping, he found the lad, perfectly well, standing in the parlor.

"Richard, what on earth is the matter?" Ellis barely held back from exploding.

"Nothing."

"Nothing? You scream like that for nothing?"

"I just called you."

Ellis searched the boy's eyes. He truly was puzzled over his uncle's reaction. Was it possible that all boys yelled like that? *Well, not in my house.*

"I thought you were hurt, Son. Sit down, please."

Richard sat on the tall, straight-back sofa. "If you need me, come find me. Don't yell."

Holding back tears, Richard nodded his head.

Ellis calmed himself down and sat beside the boy, wrapping his arm around him. "What was it you called me for?"

Richard pointed to the stereoscope on the table.

Seeing the object, Ellis said, "Would you like to look at some pictures?" Against his arm, he felt Richard trembling with fear. Ellis scooped the boy up and placed him on his lap. "I'm sorry, Richard. I didn't mean to scare you."

Richard wound his soft-skinned arms up around his uncle's neck. His blond curls buried deep into Ellis's chest. Overcome with compassion, Ellis kissed the top of Richard's head and held him tight.

❧

Bea liked Cook. At first she figured the woman for a slave, but soon her forward mannerisms revealed that wasn't the case. Whomever this woman was, she wasn't a pawn to someone else's wishes.

The limeade was refreshing, not as sweet as lemonade, yet the sour of the limes seemed a bit more gentle than that of lemons. Cook told her the limes had grown on a tree on Ellis Southard's property.

The shade of the trees around the cottage helped ease the summer-like temperatures. A gentle breeze blew through the windows. Bea loved the cottage. It was small, but wonderfully decorated, just like a captain's quarters on a ship. The wood paneling, the berth that held the bed, everything was so similar to that of the *Justice* where she had been the guest of Captain Brighton for meals during her trip from New York.

Cook's words brought her back to the present. "Your bed is made. Now remember what ol' Cook says and don't do too much today or tomorrow. Your body needs to adjust to this heat."

"Yes. Thank you."

"Dinner will be served at five. I leave to be with my family by six."

"I understand."

And Bea understood more than Cook realized. In New York the servants were ordered about. Their personal lives had no bearing on the time they were to devote to the family for whom they were employed. Their wealthy employers seldom gave thought to the possibility that their servants' families might have needs too. Here was another reason to be grateful for her parents' example. They were sensitive to their servants' needs. But in Cook's case, she seemed to be the one giving the orders. Bea grinned.

"What be on your mind, child?" Cook inquired.

"Oh, nothing."

"The devil be in you! Don't go lying to me. You had a thought, and a funny one at that."

"I like you, Cook. You know your mind."

" 'Tis true, but I've been known to speak when I should have kept my mouth shut. The Good Lord knows He has a problem with me in regards to that." Cook slowly wagged her head. "It's not like I don't try. Well, perhaps I don't. Guess I'm getting set in my ways.

"Now, stay in your chemise in the house and drink lots of fluids. Just for a day or two. You may not think it proper, but child, forget propriety. You need to become acclimated."

"Thank you, Cook. I can get over the immodesty as long as

I'm sure no one will come knocking at my door."

"Other than the child, I don't expect you to have visitors. I'll see you for dinner. . ."

"At five," they said in unison and chuckled.

Bea lay down after Cook left. She was exhausted. The heat had worn her out. Without Cook's help, she'd still be laced in a corset. Learning that they were rarely worn down here helped in her decision to leave it off for a couple of days. She took another sip of the cool limeade and rolled over for a nap.

❧

The pounding on her door woke her. "Nanna! Nanna!" Bea fumble for her housecoat and came to the door.

"Hi Richie, what's the matter?"

"Cook says it is time for dinner."

"Oh. Thanks. Tell Cook I'll be right over." Richard ran off, and Bea closed the door behind him. She fumbled to put on one of her light cotton dresses. Fortunately, she had packed a couple.

She found the house's decor tasteful, yet it had some of the strangest items she'd ever seen. The table and chairs in the dining area were of a French style, and the hutch, more of a Spanish design. Oddly enough, the eclectic blend worked. Bea wondered who had decorated the house. She'd never known a man to bother with such things.

"Miss Smith." Ellis held a chair out for her to be seated.

The trestle table was set with fine china and well-polished silver. The stemware was crystal, with flowers delicately etched on each goblet. Ellis Southard apparently had made his fortune.

"Thank you, Mr. Southard."

Ellis nodded and took his place at the head of the table.

"Can I show Nanna my room after dinner?" Richard asked.

Bea watched Ellis from the corner of her eye, sitting up straight, careful not to show too much interest. After all, the man already thought she pampered the child.

"Yes, you may, Son."

Bea was pleased to see admiration in Richard's eyes for his uncle. Perhaps he had taken some interest in the child.

❧

Cook served the dinner and sat with them at the table. It seemed odd to Bea, yet, on the other hand, perhaps it explained the familiarity with which she spoke of Ellis Southard.

"Shall we pray?" Ellis offered a brief prayer of thanksgiving.

At least he prayed over his meal, she thought. Was it possible he was a Bible-believing Christian? That would answer at least one of her prayers for Richard and his future life with his uncle.

"Cook and I often eat together, Miss Smith. She's been invited to move in and live here, but she prefers her own small cottage with relatives cluttering up the place." Ellis forked another morsel of fish.

Can the man read my mind? Bea scrutinized Ellis's blue-gray eyes, catching the hint of a smile within them. Her heart warmed a bit.

"Mr. Southard, you know that isn't the way of it. I'm the elder of the family and they expect me to keep the order."

"Now, Cook, your son is old enough to be the elder. You just like telling folks what they ought to do."

Bea found the playful bantering comforting and informative.

"Nanna," Richard broke in. "Uncle Ellis bought me a fishing pole and he said we could go fishing."

"That's wonderful, Richie."

"Richie?" Ellis whispered the question.

"I'm sorry. Richard," Bea corrected herself. She needed to remember this man was very formal.

"Richie seems a fine name for the boy," Cook muttered, and played with a morsel of fish on her plate.

"Nanna always calls me Richie."

"Enough," Ellis snapped.

Bea fought back a surge of anger. She did not intend to have this child raised by a brute. She saw no cause for him to bellow.

Ellis continued. "If you wish to be called 'Richie' by Miss

Smith that is fine."

Cook quickly finished her meal. Bea hustled down the rest of her dinner in silence. No sense lingering and possibly angering Mr. Southard again. Richard excused himself from the table as soon as he swallowed his last bite. He walked around and stood by Bea's side.

"Nanna, can I show you my room now?"

"Yes, I would like that."

Bea couldn't retreat up the stairs fast enough. Richard slipped his tiny hand in hers. She cherished his touch, and her heart tightened again. How could she possibly live without him?

Richie's quarters seemed to shout out, "boy's room." Intrigued by the fact that Ellis had managed to acquire a few toys, she found herself suddenly wobbly and confused. Perhaps it was the heat? She sat down on the bed and patted it. "Richie, bring me a book and I'll read to you."

He grabbed one of his favorites. "Nanna, I want to sleep with you tonight."

Bea kissed the top of his head. "Oh Richie, you'll be fine in your new room. Didn't your uncle Ellis say you can look over to my cottage from your window?"

"Yes."

"I've got an idea. What if I place a candle in my window for you to see? Then you'll know I'm there."

Richard simply nodded.

"I love you, Richie."

"I love you, Nanna." He turned in her arms and embraced her hard. He was scared. This would be the first night he didn't have her close by his side. She held him tight. It would be the first night in four years she wouldn't be close to his side either. *Oh Lord, thanks for this time of embracing.* She swallowed her tears, not allowing them to flow.

"Nanna?"

"Yes, Richard."

"Can you sing 'In Peace' for me?"

"Sure, honey." And Bea began to sing the familiar Bible verse she had turned into a lullaby so many years before.

> "In peace I will both lie down and sleep.
> For thou alone, oh Lord,
> makest me to dwell in safety.
> Psalms four: eight."

Ellis stood just outside Richard's doorway, his heart heavy like a sack of salt. Compassion for this woman and his nephew overwhelmed him. How could he separate them? They truly loved and cared for one another. *She's the only mother the boy has ever known,* he realized. Elizabeth died when Richard was barely one. So much death for such a small child.

He shouldn't have snapped at the dinner table. His words with Cook after they departed were not pleasant. She chastised him on his behavior. How could he explain that he was still having a hard time dealing with the loss of his brother? They had been close as children, and had corresponded constantly as adults. He knew Richard's intimate thoughts about war and the massive destruction of humanity he had seen. He knew how such things had grieved his brother.

He also knew that Richard had a problem being home alone with his son—that he saw his beloved wife etched in his features—that each glance brought back the painful memory of her death and rekindled his guilt for having gone to fight the accursed war. Ellis knew all the secret thoughts of a man unable to cope with his wife's death. His brother had even been tempted to just leave the child in his nanny's care and head for the western frontier. And yet there were other times when responsibility and duty were paramount in his brother's life. He had planned to train young Richard to run the farm, teach him business and how to turn a profit.

Ellis eventually concluded that war played havoc with a man's mind. He wished never to partake in such an event. He had been in Key West when Florida seceded from the Union and when the Union soldiers took over Fort Zachary Taylor. The captain ordered all those sympathetic with the South off the island, and the rest were given the option to stay on the island and not fight. Thankfully, few left the island before the orders to leave were rescinded.

Ellis never had to fight. He'd never been forced to take sides. Now that the war was over, the island was beginning to recover financially from its losses.

The beauty of Bea's voice lulled him away from his thoughts as he watched her caress the gentle blond strands of Richard's hair. He longed for a woman to stroke him with such a loving caress.

How long had it been? Ten? No, fifteen years since he walked away from Heather, her father, and his shotgun. They had been foolish young people who thought they were in love, only to discover it was simply infatuation. Had it been love, he would have returned for her when he was older and brought her to live with him. Instead, once out of her sight, her memory, their "love" had grown cold.

No, he was not a man to be trusted with a beautiful woman. He groaned inwardly and left them to their own loving union.

four

The warm glow of morning sunlight lapped the palm fronds outside her window as a rooster crowed. Bea ached to be with Richard. This was the first time since his birth she hadn't been at his side, the first morning she wasn't in the kitchen making breakfast for him. She felt useless. She snuggled back under the sheet, having discarded the other bedcovers within minutes of retiring last evening. The small nub of a candle remained on her windowsill. She'd let it burn far longer than needed, just in case Richie would call out for her.

Needed her? She snickered. "He's adjusting just fine with his uncle, Lord. I'm the one who is having a hard time with it. Perhaps I should return home."

She waited for some earth-shattering revelation to bellow from the heavens. At this point she'd even settle for that still small voice spoken of in the Bible. Something, anything. She needed advice, direction. Her world was collapsing and the only verse of Scripture that seemed to placate her was Ecclesiastes 3:5, "A time to embrace. . ."

Disgusted with her self-remorse, Bea flung the sheet off and sprang out of bed. The room spun. She sat back down on the bed, clasping the edge of the mattress for balance. Her body trembled uncontrollably. Her hands felt clammy. What was happening to her? She closed her eyes. Her head began to pound.

She'd lived through hot weather before. Cook said to stay in her chemise and she had. So why was she so unsteady on her feet?

Beatrice's shaky hand grasped the water glass beside her bed and slowly lifted it to her mouth. Snow hadn't fallen yet back home in upstate New York, but she knew the pond was icing over. In a week's time she'd gone from freezing temperatures to sweltering heat. She dipped her handkerchief in the basin and dampened her brow.

Perhaps she should remain in bed. Bea eased her body slowly back upon the mattress. "Oh Lord, help me, I'm so dizzy and weak," she mumbled in prayer, then closed her eyes and collapsed into the cool darkness of her mind.

❧

Ellis couldn't get over Richard's constant chattering. Questions, he had a million of them. Carefully, he answered them one at a time. Richard was a handsome child, and his eyes were so penetrating. When those eyes looked at him, Ellis felt as if they pierced his soul.

"Uncle Ellis?"

"Yes, Richard?" Ellis scooped another section of passion fruit from its yellow rind.

Richard held up his half-section of the fruit and asked, "What's this called?"

"They call it passion fruit. Some, I've heard, call it grapefruit."

"That's silly."

"Why?"

"Because it doesn't look like a grape, and it's much bigger."

Ellis chuckled. "I suppose you're right, Son."

"Uncle Ellis?"

"Yes, Richard."

"How come Nanna isn't having breakfast with us?"

"I don't know. Perhaps she overslept this morning."

"But Nanna always is up before I am."

It was odd that Beatrice hadn't come over for breakfast. He had told her the precise time for meals, and she was expected to join them. "Possibly she's tired from the heat."

"How come it's so hot here?" Richard asked, working his spoon back and forth until the fruit spit at him.

"Because this part of the earth is closer to the sun."

"How come?"

"I don't know, other than that's the way the Good Lord made it."

"Oh." Richard popped a seed out of his fruit.

"Uncle Ellis?"

Ellis didn't think he'd ever heard his named called out as many times as this lad had called him in the past hour. "What is it, Son?"

He held up the large seed. "If I plant this seed will it grow?"

"I reckon so. Would you like to do that?"

Richard's blue eyes sparkled with excitement. "Can I?"

"Sure, but we need to let the seed dry for a day or two first."

"We had to do that with the corn.

"Uncle Ellis, did you live at my daddy's farm when you were a boy?"

"I sure did. Even helped plant some corn."

"How come I never saw you?"

Out of the mouths of innocent children, Ellis inwardly lamented. "I was busy here with my sponge business."

"How do you grow sponges? Do you plant seeds like corn?"

If he answered that question, he'd be late for certain. Ellis wiped his mouth with a cloth napkin. "Richard, I'd love to tell you all about sponge-fishing, but if I don't get to work, my men will not go to work, and work is what pays to put the food on the table and roof over our heads. So maybe we can revisit this later?"

"All right." Richard grabbed his napkin, wiped his mouth and hands, and promptly stood. "Where do we go to work?"

The boy intended to go to work with him. Ellis took in a deep breath. He needed a break. But he wanted to be accessible for the child.

"Richard," Cook called. "I need you to go and visit your Nanna."

Ellis didn't pass up the opportunity. "Would you look after Nanna today? I'm sure she's having trouble with this heat. You'd be a big help to me if you kept an eye on her."

"All right." Richard scurried out of the dining hall, his feet pattering down the hall.

"Thanks, Cook." Ellis turned to her and smiled.

"The boy is most curious, I'd say. But he's a smart one. Truth be told, I'm worried about Miss Smith. She should have been up here by now. I haven't seen any movement in the house. I'm a bit concerned."

"She'll need your care today. Can you handle the child as well?"

Cook raised her hands to her ample hips. "Now who do you think cared for my young 'uns?"

Ellis held back a grin. He'd known she'd rise to the challenge. But if he had asked her straight out, she would have given him an hour-long lecture about how she wasn't "hired to be no nanny."

"Now, you take that smirk right off your face. I know what you be thinkin'. Besides, I like the gal."

Ellis chuckled and left before anyone could cause him further delay. He was already a half-hour late, though he'd still arrive before his men.

❧

"Nanna! Nanna!"

Bea heard the pounding at her door. She even heard Richie calling her. Yet try as she might, she couldn't roll her body out of bed. Every time she tossed herself over to her side she became dizzy. Her voice was weak.

"Richie," she breathed. Could he hear her? *"Oh God, help me."*

❧

"Uncle Ellis, help!" His nephew's scream reached his ears just as he rounded the gate. "Help!"

Beatrice. . .Miss Smith. . .trouble. Ellis turned back and ran toward the cottage.

Richard stood outside the door, crying. "Help, Uncle Ellis, Nanna won't come."

Ellis lifted the iron latch and flung open the door. He rushed toward the bedroom and found Beatrice wrapped in her bed-sheet. "Richard, go get Cook."

"Is she all right?"

"She will be, Son. Please, go get Cook."

Thankfully, Richard didn't have any more questions. Beatrice was as red as a cooked lobster, and he knew what that meant. She needed to be cooled down and quickly. He reached for a rag in the basin. The water was warm. He dampened it anyway and applied it to her forehead.

The cistern will be the best place for her, he thought, his mind racing. *It should be full this time of year.* Ellis scooped her up and carried her out to the backyard, to the large coral trough protected by a weathered shed. He'd often thought the cistern was far too big, but today it would prove its worth. He sat her on the top step, her feet dangling in the pool of water. He held her in his left arm and reached into the pool to dampen the rag again. This time it would be more refreshing.

Gently he applied the cool cloth over her face and neck, her arms and legs, carefully avoiding her torso.

Cook burst into the shed, huffing and gasping for breath. "Mister Ellis, what's the matter with the poor child?"

"I'm no doctor, but I'd say she has a serious case of heat-stroke. Cool her down, Cook. Keep her cool. I'll fetch the doctor."

"I'll take care of the child," she replied, immediately taking Beatrice from Ellis, cradling her like a mother with child.

Richard stood next to Cook trembling, tears streaming down his face. "Is Nanna going to die?" he asked.

"No, Son. She's going to be just fine." Ellis knelt beside him and held his hands. *So much death in this little one's life, Lord. Please make his Nanna all right,* he silently prayed. "Would you help Cook keep Nanna wet?"

Frightened eyes stared inquiringly into his uncle's.

"She'll be fine, Richard, trust me."

Richard nodded.

Cook continued to pour the water over Beatrice's lethargic body.

"Can you help her, Son?"

"Yes."

"Good. Strip down to your shorts and stand in the water next to Cook. Keep pouring water on her. I'll get the doctor."

Richard began stripping off his clothes. Ellis figured the water would help the child as well. While he didn't appear to be having any trouble with the heat, he might later. A good dip in the cool cistern would be helpful for him. Ellis headed for town, thanking God for living in such a small community with the doctor a few blocks away.

❧

"Miss Smith."

Someone was calling her, but who? The gentle lull of a woman's voice continued to penetrate her muddled thoughts.

"Come on child, I know you can hear me."

"Nanna!" Richie cried.

Richard, crying. Beatrice opened her eyes wide and tried to bolt upright. Water? She was in a tub? With Richard? And . . .and. . .Cook? What was going on here?

Cook's warm chocolate face broke into a grin, and her eyes sparkled. "Glad to see you're feeling better."

"Where am I? What's going on?"

"A touch of the heat. Didn't drink enough, I reckon."

"Nanna!" Richie exclaimed and jumped on her. The boy was soaking wet, she quickly realized, and in this. . .this huge tub.

Bea embraced Richard. "Where am I? Where are we?"

"This here be a cistern. Folks on the island have them all over. We collect the water during the rainy season and have it for the dry season. When the troops came to the island in the twenties, folks realized they wouldn't have enough fresh water in the wells. So they built these. Come in pretty handy."

Handy—the water was downright wonderful. Beatrice gathered in her surroundings. She was sitting on a white coral step at a rectangular pool of water with walls of coral as well. A small wooden roof with short sides stood over the area with a hatch-like opening at the peak of the roof. She cupped a handful of the refreshing water and sipped. It was cool and very energizing.

"Drink slowly. Your body has had quite a shock."

"How'd I get here?"

"Mr. Southard brought you."

Bea's cheeks flamed. She was in her undergarments. "Oh my," she gasped.

"Don't be fussing about modesty now, child. He had you wrapped in a bed-sheet. I took that off."

"Oh."

"Mr. Southard is a perfect gentleman. He's gone to fetch the doctor. I reckon he'll be here shortly."

"Doctor? What happened?"

"Near as I can figure, you passed out from the heat. Your skin was bright red when I first came on you."

Bea looked at her arms. They were pink, but certainly not red.

"Your color's almost back to normal," Cook said.

Richie sat on the step beside Beatrice. "Isn't this great?" Richie wiggled his toes in the water.

Bea reached out to him, found she was still dizzy, and put her hand back down on the steps to steady herself.

"Now don't you go moving too quickly, Miss."

"I can't believe how shaky I am."

"Comes with the heat, if you don't take care of yourself. Now sit back and enjoy the water." Cook rose from her step and sat down on the top stair.

"Nanna, do you think Uncle Ellis will let me go swimming in here?"

"I doubt your uncle will want you swimming in here, child," Cook answered. "We've got a big ocean out there, plenty of water for a boy to go swimming if'n he has a mind too."

"Can I go swimming in the ocean, Nanna?"

"Give your Nanna some time to rest."

Richard's shoulders sagged. "All right."

Bea couldn't possibly keep Richard's questions straight in her mind. It took all of her energy just to try and stay awake.

❧

"She's in the cistern, Doc." Ellis pointed to the backyard shed covering the cistern.

"Quick reasoning, Ellis," Doctor Hanson replied.

"Cook and my nephew are back there with her. Unless you think you need me, I think for propriety's sake I best stay out front."

"I understand."

"Thanks, Doc. Send the boy to me. I'll take him with me to work."

"Sure." Doc Hanson headed to the backyard.

Ellis paced his front yard, picking up some fallen palm fronds and tossing them in a pile. A house, a yard, a child—all brought more burdens, and more responsibility into in his life. Not to mention a guest who had almost died. A pain shot through Ellis's chest. She had such lily-white skin, made even more beautiful by the few freckles dotting her cheeks. The woman weighed next to nothing in his arms. She didn't have the strength to even protest. Never in a million years would he forget her lifeless form draped across his arms. Why hadn't he checked on her sooner, when she hadn't appeared for breakfast?

Ellis kicked a coral rock out of his path. Life sure had changed in a little over a month. Then, he had been a man of no worries. Oh perhaps a few regarding the success of his business, but then he only had himself to provide for. His bank account grew. He had more than he needed.

He had sunk a tremendous portion of his savings into this old house—a house he had purchased upon learning he was to raise his brother's son. Oh, how the tables had turned.

He had hired Cook to fix his dinner and clean his rented room in town. The owner of the boardinghouse, Ana White, could no longer care for her boarders in that fashion, so he found Cook. In the end, Cook worked for just about everyone in the house, including Ana. She was quite a woman for her age.

He was thankful she had come to work for him here. But he knew she still wandered over to the boardinghouse and took care of a few folks there as well.

"Uncle Ellis."

Ellis spun around to see the child, dripping wet, his rumpled clothes in his arms and fear knotting his forehead.

"How is she, Son?"

"She's awake."

"Good."

"Do I have to go with you?"

How could he take the child away? "Not if you don't want to. But I thought we could walk down to the dock, speak to my workers, and come right back."

"Really?" Richard's eyes widened. A curl of a smile edged on the side of his mouth.

"Sure. Do you want to come with me or stay?"

Richard turned and looked back at the cistern. "Will she be all right?"

"Yes, Son. Cook and the doctor can handle things from here. But I'm sure you helped a great deal."

Richard puffed out his chest. "I did like you said. I got her real wet."

Ellis chuckled. "Good, Son, real good."

five

Ellis worked out the tension in his back, then walked hand in hand with Richard toward his dock. The sun was bright, the sky a vivid blue, a few clouds lining the horizon. "Richard," Ellis pointed to his right. "See those tall clouds that look like a top?"

"Uh-huh."

"Those are funnel clouds. The air is swirling around real fast."

"Really? How does it work?"

"Hmmm, tell you what. When we get to my office I'll show you how the wind spins and the cloud is formed." The ploy worked; the boy seeming to have taken his mind off his nanny. On the other hand, Ellis found himself wondering how she was doing—if they had her out of the cistern yet and back in her cottage. He'd have moved her into the house to care for her, but the cottage was actually a tad cooler than his home.

"Uncle Ellis?"

"Yes, Son."

"Did you make this dock?"

"No, I bought it from the man who built it."

"How come it's so long? New York had little docks."

The child was amazing, noticing little things like that. "In New York harbor the water becomes deep quickly. In Key West, you have to go out a long way from shore before the water gets deep, so the dock goes out to the deep water to enable the ships to come up to them."

"Oh." Richard pointed toward the mounds of sponges drying on his dock. "What are those?"

"Sponges. They grow in the ocean. My men take small boats out and dive into the water to bring up the sponges."

"Can you teach me how to swim?"

"Sure."

"Nanna plays in the pond with me at the farm. But I don't think she knows how to swim."

"Hmmm, it's possible. Growing up on the farm, I learned to swim in the pond. Is that where Nanna took you to play?"

"Yes, by the big rock."

Ellis smiled. How many leaps had he taken off that rock into the cool crisp water below? He couldn't possibly count. "The water in Key West is much warmer than back home."

"That's 'cause we are closer to the sun, right?"

Ellis grinned broadly. Richard was a very bright boy indeed. He walked his nephew to the end of his pier where he had a small building which housed his office and tools for the men. Inside he showed him the sharp knives the sponge fishermen used for tools, and the nets they tied to their waists. Some of the men preferred an odd scissors-shaped tool to the knife, depending on which method the man had been taught.

"Uncle Ellis, what's this?" Richard pointed to a long pole with a two-pronged iron hook.

"That's for hooking the sponges from inside the boat."

"Do you go sponge-fishing too?"

"Sometimes, but not too often. Most of the time I have to work in the office here, or with the sponges after they've been harvested.

"Go take a whiff of that pile of sponges over there."

Richard scurried over. He wrinkled his face and looked back at Ellis. "They stink like dead fish."

Ellis chuckled.

❧

Bea raised her head off the soft, down-feather pillow. She inhaled the freshness of the clean white sheets Cook had remade her bed with. "Cook, what were you and the doctor whispering about before he left?"

"Not worth repeatin'. He was just making sure I knew how to care for ya. I'll be spending the night with ya, too."

"I'm fine," Beatrice protested.

"Land sakes, child, you are exhausted from that heat. I've got to make sure you drink enough fluids."

"But you have a family."

"True, but the doc, he's a-sending a message to my house. My children are all grown with children of their own. They feed themselves now, since I cook dinner for Mr. Ellis, and they insists I eat with him."

"I don't mean to pry, but were you a slave?"

"No, ma'am. My family was set free when I was no higher than your knee. There's always been good pay for honest work for Bahamians on Key West. So my husband, George, brought us here right after we married. We bought our own home after a few years, and 'though things been tough at times, we've had a good life here on the island."

"What about the war?"

"Truth be told, the island wasn't much a part of the war. Granted, some of the folks who were wreckers suffered hard times when they weren't allowed to do no salvaging. And, what with the navy being here, there weren't quite so many wrecks."

"Tell me about this island of Key West. Where'd it get its name?"

"Original name was Cayo Hueso. That's Spanish for 'Island of Bones.' Folks say, for a long time the island was just a watering hole for sailors. Belonged to Cuba back then. Eventually, the king of Spain gave it to a man for faithful service. That fella, in turn, sold it to four businessmen from Connecticut. And they was the ones that started building a town here. Soon after, the navy put up a base. But 'twas the wrecking industry what brought a lot of money to the island." Cook leaned back and gave a low laugh, slapping her hands on her broad lap. "Listen to me rattle on."

"No, I'm interested, really."

Cook sat her ample figure down on a rocker beside Bea's bed. "I can tell a tale or two about this here island. It's very different from the Bahamas, but I'm most comfortable here."

Beatrice's eyes were getting heavy. "Were there pirates living here?"

"Sure. Still are."

Beatrice pulled the sheet up to her chin.

Cook's robust laughter filled the room. "Most of 'em are retired. They made their money. Now they've settled down, got married, had kids. Got respectable, you might say."

"Really?" The word slipped past Bea's lips before she could catch herself.

"Wreckers salvaged whatever was worth taking from ships. Story goes, years ago, before the law came to the island, some folks would put a light out on the water to confuse the sailors so they'd run their ships aground on the reefs."

"No."

"Don't know if it be true or not. Just know that's what some say, is all. But it woke you up, didn't it?"

Bea chuckled. "Yes."

"Good, you need to stay alert, keep drinking. Rest will come later. But the doctor wants you awake for a mite longer before you sleep again."

"All right. Perhaps you can tell me some more tales of Key West."

"Why don't you tell me something about yourself?"

"Like what?"

"Why are you a nanny at such a young age?"

"Oh, well, that's easy. My best friend was Elizabeth Southard, Richard's mother. She had a terrible time when she was with child. We weren't even sure she was going to pull through. Elizabeth decided she needed some help, and she didn't want just anyone. Richard's family was gone, so they were alone on the farm. And she, being so weak. . .well, she asked me."

"You was a good friend." Cook tapped Bea's hand and proceeded to dip a cloth in the bowl of water. "Go on, I'll keep you cool while you tell me more."

"At first I was supposed to help only until shortly after Richard was born. But Elizabeth never fully recovered. So she asked me to stay. My parents weren't too happy. They'd had my coming-out party just before Elizabeth turned ill. Nevertheless, they understood the closeness between us, and knew that, if it were me who was so desperately ill, Elizabeth would have constantly been at my side.

"Elizabeth worsened after Richard was born. She developed a cough and never shook it." A tear edged her eye. "A year after Richard's birth, she passed on. But not before begging me to stay and continue to watch over Richard. Not that she had to beg me for anything regarding that little one."

"He's a charmer," Cook agreed."You should have seen him this morning. Had his uncle tied up in knots just trying to figure out where all the boy's questions came from."

Bea laughed, her parched lips feeling brittle. She reached for a glass of Cook's refreshing limeade, noticing her hand still shook, though it was much stronger than earlier this morning. "I can't believe I fainted."

"Praise be to the Almighty! If little Richard hadn't come to check on you right away, you would have been far worse."

"He was so frightened."

"That he was, child. But the Good Lord was with us, and you're going to be fine. You should have seen him pouring the water on you. He just kept doing what his uncle Ellis told him to do. You've raised a fine lad there, Miss. You should be proud."

"Don't know that I've done all that much, really. Just loved him as if he were my own."

"It shows, child. It shows." Cook finished applying the damp cloth to Bea's limbs and sat back down on the wooden chair beside the bed. She brushed the gray hair, streaked with black, off her face. "Tell me where the child's father was during all these years."

"The war."

"How could I forget that? Mr. Ellis sure was broken up by

his brother's death. I never seen a grown man so close to someone so far away."

"Close? Elizabeth never even spoke of him."

"I've been carin' for Mr. Ellis for a number of years now. He been receivin' a letter from his brother at least once a month."

"Even during the war?"

"Truly a miracle, I say. Yes'm, he managed to get some mail out with a Captain Brighton. Seems the captain was working for the North, privateering. 'Course, you talk with a Southern sympathizer, they'd call him an outright pirate."

Bea chuckled. "I guess it all depends on which side of the war you're on." So, the *Justice's* captain was a pirate or a privateer. Interesting.

"You speak a lot of truth there, child.

"You mentioned your 'coming-out party.' Is that when your family says you're now ready for courtin' and marriage?"

Bea felt her cheeks heat up and she weakly answered, "yes."

"I'm sure you left a few men lamentin' your status as a nanny."

"I wasn't one to seek the attention of a man. Never cared to, really. I suppose I never found one that was interesting enough." Bea placed her empty glass back on the nightstand.

❧

"Uncle Ellis, who buys the sponges?" Richard asked, squatting on a tall chair beside him at his desk. Mounds of paperwork needed going over. But his mind was yet again on a hazel-eyed sea siren. His thoughts lingered on whether or not she'd survive this heat. He felt certain he had caught her before she became critical. The cistern was a true blessing from God. But he was still worried for the sake of the child. How would Richard handle losing another person close to him? Ellis shuddered and rubbed the gooseflesh off his arms.

"Uncle Ellis, can we go see Nanna now?"

Ellis plopped down his pencil. "Sure, Son. I was just thinking about her myself."

Richard's bright blue eyes smiled as he jumped off the tall chair he had been perched on. "I'm ready."

"Great, give me a minute to put these books together so I can take them home."

"Why do you write in your books? Nanna said I mustn't write in my books."

"Your Nanna is right. But these are special books for keeping track of a business's money. How much a business spends, how much it makes."

"How much money do you have, Uncle Ellis?"

"Enough." Ellis placed his large masculine hands on top of Richard's head and ruffled his curls, just like he had seen Miss Smith do on more than one occasion.

Richard smiled. "Nanna says I have a lot of money, too."

"She did, did she?" What was this woman telling this child? Why would a boy need to worry himself about money at his age? He would need to have a word with Miss Smith when she was feeling better. At least one word.

Richard nodded. "Nanna said when my mommy died she had money put in a special place for me when I became a man."

"I see."

"Nanna said it was to buy my own farm, or go places, or whatever I want."

"That is a special gift, Son."

"Nanna says a wise man thinks before he spends his money."

Maybe he wouldn't need to speak with the woman after all.

"Nanna says some men spend their money on silly things."

"I see."

"Nanna says wise money is like planting corn. If you plant it right it grows and makes more."

"Your Nanna is a pretty smart woman."

"Nanna says Grandpa Smith taught her about wise money."

"I see," he said for the third time. And perhaps he was beginning to see more than he ever expected. As the child's nanny, she was responsible for his schooling, and she knew that Richard's job would be caring for the farm one day. Maybe she wasn't as overprotective as he'd suspected.

"Uncle Ellis?"

"Yes, Son?" Ellis scooped the child into his arms, figuring they would make it home faster if he carried him. The child was a wonder, his mind so quick with facts and details. He soaked up knowledge like his sponges soaked up water. He was a remarkable lad who had a remarkable teacher. Ellis pondered the possibility of asking a certain Miss Beatrice Smith to stay on as the child's nanny. Of course, he'd probably have to offer her holidays to visit with her family in New York. . . Still, the idea was plausible.

"Who taught you about money?"

"My dad and your father."

"Was my daddy wise with money?"

"Yes."

Richard nodded. A somber expression creased his delicate face. "I miss my daddy."

Ellis swallowed back a gasp. He hadn't expected Richard to be so honest with his emotions.

Ellis paused in the street. He lowered the child down and knelt before him, face-to-face. "I do too, Son. I do too."

six

"Nanna!" Richard cried from the doorway of her cottage.

"Come in here, Richie, I'm laying down."

"All right."

The old wooden rocking chair creaked as Cook eased herself up. "I'm going to speak with Mr. Ellis, Miss. I'll be back in a minute."

Beatrice nodded. Richard stood by her bed. She tapped the covers. "Come on up."

He climbed up and sat beside her. Bea wrapped her arm lovingly around him.

"Are you okay?" he asked.

"I'll be fine. I feel silly for not drinking as much as I should have for this heat."

"Uncle Ellis said you'd be all right."

"I'll need to stay in bed the rest of the day, but perhaps tomorrow we can get to your lessons."

"Nanna, I can play tomorrow so you can rest more."

Bea chuckled. "I'll see that your lessons are fun. Tell me, did you go to work with your uncle Ellis?"

Enthusiastically he nodded his head. "He fishes for sponges and they stink like dead fish. Uncle Ellis says he washes them so they don't smell."

"Interesting." *Sponges and the other natural wonders this island brings will make exciting lessons for Richard and myself,* Bea thought. Then she remembered she wouldn't be teaching Richard for much longer. Bea fought back her discouragement and tried concentrating on what Richard was telling her. Something about Ellis writing in his books.

". . .Uncle Ellis says he writes his money in a book."

"You mean keeps track of his money in his books. That's

good, he uses his money like a good farmer."

"I told him about corn money."

"You did?"

"Uh-huh."

Bea smiled. The man probably thought she was a fool for putting money in the terms of seeds, but it seemed like the best way to explain it to a four year old.

Cook walked in with a broad smile. "Richard, I think you need to let your Nanna rest. You best go with your uncle now."

Richard nodded and slid off the bed. " 'Bye, Nanna. I'll come later."

" 'Bye, Richie. You mind your uncle, and I'll be up tomorrow."

"All right." He ran from the room.

"Now, I say you close those heavy eyes of yours and get some rest. I'll wake you later for some more to drink and maybe a light broth." Cook applied the damp cloth over her body again.

Bea struggled to keep her eyes open. Perhaps she should rest for a moment. Slowly she let them close, the burning at the back of her lids finding relief. So tired, so exhausted, she needed sleep. . . .

❧

Bea awoke to Cook's delicate touch.

"Good morning, child. You slept well."

"I feel better, but still weak."

"You'll be that way for most of the day. You rest and start getting some good food into your body. Hopefully, you'll be feeling better by evening."

Beatrice grasped Cook's soft, leathered hands. "Thank you." No other words fit. She was deeply indebted to this woman, this stranger who no longer seemed a stranger, but a friend.

"You're welcome. Don't you be carryin' on about how much I did. Just watched over you is all. Any good Christian woman would have."

"I don't know what I would have done without you."

"You would have been stuck with Mr. Ellis pacing all night and young Richard wanting to sleep with you to make sure you were all right."

She grinned at the image of Richie cradled beside her in bed. They had shared many lonely nights that way. However, she couldn't quite figure why Mr. Ellis, as Cook called him, would be pacing the floor on account of her. As far as he was concerned, she was an over-protective nursemaid who would need to return home on the first possible ship. Her grin slipped into a rigid slim line.

"Did you sleep at all, Cook?"

"Some. I'm fine, child. But if you be fine, I'm going to the house to fix up some breakfast. What would you like?"

"Nothing. I still don't feel like eating."

"Hurumph. You'll be eating something. I'll make it light. Lay back down; I'll return shortly."

"Thank you." Bea watched Cook waddle out of her room. There would be no denying that woman. If she brought you something to eat, you'd better eat it. Cook's ways brought back memories of an old school matron, Miss Arno. The woman was not one to trifle with. She bellowed orders and you followed, or you were left cleaning boards, desks, floors, windows, anything the woman could think of. Bea shook her head and attempted to get up.

Slowly she draped her feet over the side of the bed. She waited for the dizziness to return. Thank the Good Lord there was none. Feeling a bit more sure of herself, she eased her feet to the floor and continued holding the edge of the mattress. Carefully she straightened up. Her legs wobbled, her body felt exhausted. Should she dare take a couple steps to sit in the old wooden rocker?

Tentatively she lifted her right foot and slid it forward. Then her left. Yes, she could make it. She would just need to be careful. Easing herself into the rocker, she clasped her hands in her lap and proceeded with her morning prayers. She had a lot to be thankful for this morning, and a lot to petition the Lord about as well.

As always, Richard was in the forefront of all her prayers. "Father God, You know my heart, You know my love for this child. If there is any way I could remain on as his nanny, I'd appreciate it. But I do trust him into Your hands and Your protection for him. You are the Creator, and You do know what's best for him. I'm trying to refrain from embracing, to let go and trust him to You, removing myself. But it is difficult, Father. I love him so."

❧

Ellis groaned as he dragged his body out of bed. He'd been up most of the night. Finally, Cook had told him not to come back to the cottage again; she needed some rest too. Then, the nagging torment that he was ultimately responsible for the nanny's condition kept his eyes from closing while his feet wore out the floorboards. She was doing well, fortunately. She would recover. But he couldn't forgive himself for having been so insensitive. He had a pretty clear understanding of the amount of undergarments a woman wore up north, and this heat was not fit for a lady of such refinement. Many of the wives of the local residents refused to live here year-round because of the heat. But that number was changing as the women developed a taste for Spanish clothing, a far more agreeable attire for this climate.

A disheveled face in the mirror stared back at him, his eyes bloodshot from the lack of sleep. His beard needed a good trimming and brushing. He worked the stray hairs with his hand into a some semblance of order. Hoping the water would revive him, he rinsed his face one more time.

Ellis worked his way down the stairs to make breakfast for everyone, feeling it was the least he could do. Cook needed some rest too, having been up most of the night herself. Of course, some of that was due to his wandering over there half a dozen times to check on Miss Smith's condition.

"What are you doing here?" he barked, seeing Cook busy at the stove.

"I'm fixin' breakfast."

"You should be with Miss Smith, Cook. I'll fix breakfast."

"Don't you be bellowing at me, Sir. Beatrice is fine. I appreciate your offer to make the morning meal but. . ."

"Sorry, Cook," Ellis apologized.

"The lady needs something she can get down, not your idea of a breakfast," Cook teased.

Ellis raised a hand to his chest, feigning injury. *"Moi?"*

"Don't be using no fancy talk. You know you can't cook, that's why you hired me."

"I must have been out of my mind," Ellis mumbled. He truly loved Cook. She kept him in order. But, at times, the woman had an attitude which could make a man's toes curl.

"Probably so, but the Good Lord knew you needed me in your life," Cook admonished.

Ellis chuckled. "You're quite a handful, Cook. How did your husband manage?"

"Quite well, thank you," she winked in reply. "Mr. Ellis," Cook lowered her voice, "Bea is going to be fine. She had a good night. She looks well this morning. Another day of rest and she'll be fit as an oyster in its shell."

"Thanks for all your help, Cook. I don't know what I would have done."

"Found some other lady to take care of her, I'm certain. But God doesn't put people in the wrong place at the wrong time. Remember that, Mr. Ellis. She's not here by mistake."

"But. . ."

"But nothin'. God knows, God controls, if you let Him."

Duly admonished, Ellis left the breakfast preparations in the capable hands of Cook. She was right as always. If he genuinely trusted God, he shouldn't have been so worried and shouldn't have been so riddled with guilt. God had placed Beatrice Smith in the position of caring for his nephew, and He knew that they would be coming to live with him in these tropical temperatures. So why was he still blaming himself?

Because if he hadn't commited that act in the past, he would have gone home and picked up his nephew. But fear of entering his hometown, the threat of arrest, the threat of disgracing the family name and losing the farm. . .he simply couldn't risk it. So, was it ultimately still his fault that Beatrice Smith was sick?

Ellis worked the tension out of the back of his neck. "Perhaps not," he spoke to his empty office. But, just maybe, he was still responsible.

"Uncle Ellis, can I go see Nanna now?" Richard yelled down the hall.

When was that child going to learn not to yell? Ellis took a deep breath. Now was not the time to chastise him. He stepped into the hall just as Richard rounded the corner at a run to head into his office.

"Ugh!" Ellis groaned.

"Sorry. Can I?" Richard implored sheepishly.

"Yes, go right in and see how she's doing. Tell her Cook will bring breakfast shortly."

"All right." Richard turned to walk away, then paused, looking over his shoulder, and said, "Good morning, Uncle Ellis."

Ellis broke into a wide grin. "'Morning, Son. Now shoo." At that, the boy was off, running down the hall, slipping on one small carpet but handling the corner without falling. *Did I run that much when I was a boy?* he wondered. He had no memory of it. He ran outside, of course, but in the house? Nah, he couldn't have. His mother would have tanned his hide. Come to think of it. . .Ellis rubbed his backside. . .maybe she had.

❧

Bea heard the patter of Richard's feet long before she heard him call, preceded by the slam of the screen door.

"Nanna."

"Come in, Richard. I'm in my room." She straightened the sheet modestly over herself.

"Hi. Uncle Ellis said I could come over."

"I'm glad you came."

"Are you better?"

"Yes, thanks."

"Are you allowed to sit in a chair?"

"I believe so, why do you ask?"

"'Cause yesterday you had to stay in bed. Doctor said so."

"True, but I can sit up for a while now. Would you like me to read you a story?"

Richard nodded his head.

"Do you want to pick out a book or should I?"

"Can we do the story after breakfast?"

"Sure."

"Cook's making bacon." Richard's eyes sparkled.

"We can read after you have your bacon." As much as Bea enjoyed bacon, she couldn't imagine eating something so greasy at the moment. She silently prayed Cook would not ask her to.

"Nanna?"

"Yes, Richie."

He placed his small hands on his hips and stood with his feet slightly apart. "Are you drinking?"

Bea couldn't help but giggle. "Yes, Son. I'm drinking my juice."

He shook his finger. "Cook said you need to keep drinking or you'll get sick."

"I know. I'll be careful, I promise."

Richard gave one swift nod of the head and relaxed his stance. If Cook was having this effect on the child already, Ellis Southard would have his hands full raising the boy. "Do you think you better go back to the house for your breakfast? I think I can smell the bacon now."

Richard sniffed the air. His smile blossomed. "I'll be back, Nanna," he said, then spun around, and ran out the door.

The boy was always running. Beatrice wondered if his father had been a runner as well, or his uncle.

His uncle. The image of the man brought a shiver down her spine. He was so handsome, and she was so infuriatingly attracted to him. Maybe she shouldn't ask to stay on as the child's nanny. She probably should go home and do as the

Lord says, "refrain from embracing," to let little Richard go on to be the man he was meant to become. Staying in Key West would mean staying next to temptation, and Bea wasn't all that sure she could handle it.

It would be different, she thought, if she had fancied herself interested in some boys when she was younger. But they were just silly creatures, boys were. They often would start behaving like roosters near a hen house trying to get a woman's attention. Such silliness did not endear her to the male part of the species. Grown men, however, like her father, were acceptable. They either outgrew this boyish behavior or, like her father, had not been given to such childishness. She wondered if she dared ask. Her brother hadn't been one given to such nonsense until Abigail Wilson moved into town. Around her, he degenerated into 'one of the roosters.'

Bea tossed her head from side to side. Young boys like Richard didn't seem to have this problem. She wondered if it had anything to do with coming of age. Perhaps she would never know. She certainly wouldn't be around when young Richard would be turning sixteen.

A rap sounded at her door. "Miss Smith."

Bea flushed. She was naked, well maybe not naked exactly, but close enough. "Mr. Southard, I'm not presentable. Please do not come in."

"I. . .I. . .mean you no disrespect ma'am. I just wanted to let you know that I'm going to work now. Cook will be here and calling on you often. Richard will be in Cook's care, but I've given him permission to visit you as often as you wish today."

"Thank you, sir. I'm certain I'll be about tomorrow."

"Take the time to recover, Miss Smith. We don't want a repeat of yesterday." His words were almost kind, but there was a slight edge of anger in them too, she suspected.

"I'm drinking regularly and getting my rest, thank you." Regular enough that she thought she could float away if she didn't stop soon.

"Fine," he coughed. "Good day, Miss Smith."

"Good day, sir."

She wondered again if Ellis Southard truly was as cold as he appeared. What had Cook said earlier? That he would have kept her up all night with his pacing? Was he truly concerned about her? If so, he was a kind man with a cold exterior, Bea noted to herself. That was it. A man with a tender heart, who hid it well, she reasoned.

"Miss Bea," Cook called as she entered the house. "I've got some tea and some white rice for you."

"Rice?"

"Best thing to keep you from dehydrating. Problem some folks have with a new area is the water isn't the same as back home. They, hmm, well, they. . ."

"I understand." And Bea had. The Key West water was already having that "cleansing" affect on her body.

"Black tea, white rice, best medicine there is for diarrhea."

"Thanks, I think." Was there anything her body would get used to about this area? Maybe it didn't matter. Fact was, she wouldn't be staying all that long. But she wanted to be her best for the last days she spent with Richard. "Father, God, please help me get well and stay well," she moaned.

seven

The next morning Bea woke to the gentle lull of exotic bird-song outside her window. She quietly watched them flit from branch to branch, their vivid colors as beautiful and enchanting as they were different from their cousins in the North. This truly felt as if she were in a whole new world.

Today, perhaps, she could explore this tropical wonder. But would Cook allow her the pleasure? On the other hand, would her body survive it? "What could it hurt, Lord, to walk a few blocks to the center of town?" Without waiting for an answer, her thoughts skipped ahead to the quaint stores filled with merchandise to explore.

Even Ellis Southard's sponge business was so uniquely Caribbean, she reflected, as she climbed out of bed to get ready for the day. She picked up the personal sponge Cook had given her for bathing. After the very first use her skin had felt smoother, cleaner, and softer than she remembered it feeling in years.

Working into the most lightweight outfit she could find, she thought about purchasing some of the Spanish-style skirts and blouses like the ones Cook wore. They looked so comfortable.

Although she wouldn't purchase many. The island clothing would be totally unacceptable back home. There a woman was to always be properly dressed. And while Cook quite naturally wore this new casual apparel, Bea was certain the women of her social class never would, even in these tropical temperatures.

Fortunately, no one here knew of Bea's northern social status, so no heads would turn when and if she wore those outfits. What mattered was to stay covered and cool and to avoid another touch of heatstroke. In her few remaining days with

Richard, she wanted to be fit and able to enjoy the merriment and wonder of seeing this place for the first time.

Perhaps she was a bit jealous of the time Ellis played with Richard each evening before he went to bed. She'd heard them laughing and longed to be in the middle of such joyous activity. Each night she had lit the candle in her window for Richard, although Cook had been the keeper of the flame in her weakened state.

She watched from behind her closed screen door as Ellis Southard marched proudly off to work. His broad shoulders straight and firm, he walked with confidence but didn't strut with arrogance. His beard seemed shorter, more groomed this morning, its red highlights seemed to beam his contentment with life and his job.

"Snap out of it, woman," Bea chastised herself. "Why am I longing so much for this man, a stranger?" She prayed with her head bent low. "We've spoken maybe ten minutes in the three days I've been here. Well, perhaps a few more than ten. But it's been nothing, Lord. I barely know him and yet I'm attracted to him. Why? It must be the heat. Help me keep my mind together, Lord. Don't allow me to turn into some silly, swooning female."

Now what was it she had been thinking before she saw Ellis. . .Mr. Southard. . .she amended. "Ah yes, shopping." Bea opened the screen door and headed toward the main house. It was her first time in the house since falling ill. Cook had brought all her meals to the cottage, with Richard's help of course. She smiled at the thought. He was so proud, being able to help care for her. Bea's eyes started to water. "How am I going to leave this child, Lord?" she whispered.

❧

"Come on, men, let's get out there before the day is half over," Ellis hollered at his crew lounging on wood blocks and crates scattered around the dock. A few groaned, but all got up and shuffled over to the small boats that would sail out to fetch the sponges. The nets empty, a couple men per boat, he had a good business.

" 'Morning, Ellis, I see your crew has expanded." Ellis turned to see Marc Dabny approach, wearing his usual Union blue army slacks, though he had retired from the military right after the war to live on the island. His premature balding head glistened in the morning sunlight.

" 'Morning, Marc. What can I do for you?"

"Heard your nephew's come to live with you." Marc stopped his approach a couple feet away from Ellis.

"That's right, he's a great kid."

Marc looked down at his feet and cleared his throat. "Heard his nanny came with him too."

Ellis examined the man more closely. What was he after?

"Yes," he admitted.

"I was wondering if I could. . .well, if I could come and call upon the lady."

What? How dare the man!

On the other hand, Marc had been raised to seek out the gal's father to request permission to court. But he wasn't Beatrice's father, wasn't even close. Still, Beatrice was a guest in his home, and he supposed folks naturally assumed she was now working for him as the child's nanny. But he certainly didn't want to declare open hunting season for Beatrice Smith.

"Marc, the lady's been ill. Stricken with a bad case of heatstroke. By the time she's strong again, I imagine she'll be on a ship heading North."

"She won't be staying?"

"No, sir." He handled that well, he thought. Didn't lie, but didn't make her available either. "And given the severity of her heatstroke, I imagine she's anxious to leave this place."

"Heard she was a looker. And I've been wanting to settle down now since the war is over. You know, get married, and have a handful of kids. Besides, havin' a woman who's pleasant to look at wouldn't be a bad way to spend the rest of your life." Marc winked.

Ellis's stomach flip-flopped. The man wasn't looking for a companion. He was looking for a nursemaid plus a few wifely benefits. That certainly didn't describe Beatrice Smith, who was excellent with children, and had a sharp mind. She needed a man with whom she could have a relationship, not be some prize—used whenever the prizewinner suited.

"Afraid that wouldn't be Miss Smith. I believe she has family waiting on her back home." That was also not untrue, but he really hadn't talked with her about it, just assumed. In fact, he knew next to nothing about Beatrice Smith and her family. Everything he knew was through the eyes of his nephew—his love for her, and the things she'd taught him. No, he really didn't know the woman at all.

"Well, I figured I should ask you first. Didn't know if you had other plans for the lady. Didn't want to ask the lady and upset you."

"I appreciate it, Marc, but like I say, she's not staying."

"Mind if I try and persuade her anyway?"

The man deserved some credit for his persistence.

Besides, do I really have the right to say who could or could not court Miss Smith? Ellis felt like he ought to, but knew he didn't. "I don't suppose I could stop you from approaching her, but please give her another day to recover. I was quite concerned at first that she wouldn't even make it."

"Thank you. I come from a long line of Dabnys who've been known to have a way with women. So don't be too surprised if the lady decides to stay right here in Key West."

No matter what Marc Dabny thought about his family heritage, Ellis couldn't see Beatrice Smith on this man's arm. On the other hand, not being a woman himself, he didn't have a clue as to what a lady would find appealing.

"I won't be keeping you from your work, just felt I ought to speak with you first. I know we don't run on pomp and circumstance down here, but since you and I both hail from the North, I thought I'd better ask."

"I appreciate it. Have a good day, Marc."

"Adios," Marc answered in Spanish. The blend of Spanish and English added to the island's uniqueness.

Ellis worked his shoulders in circles trying to ease the tension that had stiffened his back.

Four days. The woman had been here for only four days and the vultures were already swarming. Ellis shook his head as he walked to his office. Of course, given Miss Beatrice Smith's beauty, it was a wonder no one had approached him days ago. Maybe the fact that she was so ill had made it through the island gossip chain and had kept the pursuers at bay. In any case, she was fair game for the men of Key West, and he had no right to do anything about it.

Frustrated, he absentmindedly worried his lower lip. Why did the thought bother him? Wasn't it possible that some man on Key West might be Beatrice Smith's future husband? She certainly would make a man a good wife and mother, or at least it appeared that way. But the very idea of Marc Dabny pursuing her made him tense. Marc seemed like a decent enough sort on the surface. He was respectable and followed his orders. He wouldn't make a bad husband, Ellis supposed. But then again, Marc wasn't looking for a woman who would challenge him as a man, he was looking for someone to clean his house, cook his food, and bear his children.

Ellis rubbed his temples. This was going nowhere. He wasn't Beatrice Smith's keeper. The woman could court anyone she had a mind to. It wasn't his concern. His concern was providing for his nephew and bringing him up in a manner that would have made the boy's father proud. And to do that he needed to get to work and stop this lollygagging.

❧

"Nanna, are you all right?" Richard questioned.

Bea's legs shook. Her arms felt prickly, as if being stabbed with lots of tiny needles all at once. "I feel a bit weak."

Richard ran to the house they were in front of and banged on the door. An older woman with graying hair came to the door. "May I help you?"

"Nanna doesn't feel well. Can she sit down?"

"Oh gracious, bring her here, child."

Bea didn't know whether to be proud or embarrassed by Richard's actions. They hadn't gone a quarter of a mile, but she had apparently gone too far. Richard helped her up the stairs onto the woman's porch.

"Sit in the rocker, dear, I'll fetch you some water."

"Thank you." Beatrice sat down on the wooden rocker facing the street. A small front porch with a wooden floor and white painted handrail stretched across the front of the house. A couple steps and you were to the door.

"Nanna, I'll get Uncle Ellis."

The last thing she needed was to have Ellis Southard come to her rescue. "I'll be fine. No sense worrying your uncle."

"What about Cook? She's closer." Richard's worried eyes pleaded with her to let him help.

"Come here, Richie." She scooped him up and placed him on her lap. She worked his wonderful blond curls from his face with her right hand. "I'm fine, really. I just wasn't up for this yet."

"Nanna, I don't want you to be sick."

"I'm getting better. I just have to be patient and wait for my body to recover a bit more."

"All right." Richard snuggled his head into her chest.

Bea looked up at the sound of the screen door swinging on old hinges to see the elderly woman coming out with a tall glass of lemonade. "Here you go, Miss," she said, steadying herself with her free hand on the back of Bea's chair.

Bea clasped her fingers around the glass. "Thank you." Carefully she brought it to her lips and sipped. How perfectly embarrassing to weaken in such a short amount of time. At mid-morning, the full intensity of the heat wouldn't peak for two to three hours yet.

Bea's hostess sat down in the wicker chair to her left. "My name is Vivian. You're new here aren't you, dear?"

Bea nodded her head.

"Nanna and I came from New York on a big ship. We're living with my uncle Ellis."

"With those steel-blue eyes, I should have noticed you were Mr. Southard's nephew."

Richard looked at Bea in bewilderment.

"Miss. . .I'm afraid I don't know your last name," Bea flushed.

"Sorry, its Matlin. Mrs. Joseph Matlin."

Bea nodded. "Richard, Mrs. Matlin noticed your eyes have the same coloring as your uncle Ellis's."

"Oh. That's because my daddy and uncle Ellis are brothers."

Vivian chuckled. "That's generally how it works, Son. Can I give you something to drink, and a sweet biscuit perhaps?"

"Can I, Nanna?"

"Sure." Vivian took Ellis by the hand and led him into her home. A cool breeze blew across the porch, and Bea laid her head back on the chair and closed her eyes to let the refreshing air sweep across her face. Cook had warned her to be careful, and a race to the corner of the street had clearly exceeded her limits.

She could still feel the pulse in her legs, beat after beat, protesting her stupidity. She hadn't exerted herself that much, having let Richard win. Yet she had done far more than her body could apparently handle. *How long does it take to recover from heatstroke?* she wondered.

Vivian came back out with a small china plate, with Richard in tow. "Would you like one, dear?"

Bea wasn't really hungry, but the biscuits did smell good. "Thank you, I'm sorry to impose upon you in such a way."

"It's no trouble at all, dear." Vivian sat back down on the chair opposite Beatrice and straightened her apron. "All I know is that you serve as Richard Southard's nanny. I don't know your name, dear."

"Forgive me. . .Beatrice Smith. . .heatstroke seems to be affecting me in more ways than one."

"I know what you mean, Beatrice. May I call you Beatrice?"

"Bea is fine. Have you ever suffered with this ailment?" Bea wiped the crumbs from her lap.

"Years ago, when I first came here. Came about the same time of year as you. The first week was very difficult."

"A whole week? I'll be on a ship back to New York by the end of a week. I do want to take in some of the sights prior to my departure." *Maybe the Good Lord just doesn't want me in this climate and I shouldn't get comfortable here.* Another lesson in learning to refrain from embracing, embracing a new way of life, a new culture, a new environment. It wasn't her time, and she just needed to accept the fact that she was to return home to New York.

❧

At the end of the workday Ellis returned home for his evening meal and found the house quiet.

"Hello? Anyone home?" Not a sound. *That's odd,* he thought, and proceeded to clean up and change from his work clothes into something casual. From his bedroom window he could see Cook, Richard, and Miss Smith sitting under the shade of the large banyan tree. Even from this distance Beatrice seemed pale, weak, and sorrowful. The woman was so vulnerable, so frail, and yet showed a remarkable ability to hold her own in adversity. Could this change in her demeanor be from the heatstroke?

Ellis slipped his arms into the sleeves of a cool cotton shirt, buttoning it as he made his way down the hall to the stairs and out through the kitchen to the back door. "I wondered where all of you were."

"Uncle Ellis!" Richard declared, jumping up from his spot and scampering over to him. Ellis smiled. *Well, the boy runs outside as well as inside,* he mused.

"Just takin' in the cool night air," Cook said. "The butcher got some fresh beef from Cuba, so we're having steak tonight. You're cooking on the outside grill," Cook teased, and sat farther back in her chair, putting her feet up on the one abandoned by Richard.

Fresh beef was a rarity on the island, and he'd given Cook a standing order that anytime there was a shipment she should purchase some.

"I see." Ellis hoisted Richard up on his shoulders. "Come on, Son. It's our night to cook for the ladies."

At the back of the yard he lifted Richard off his shoulders and placed him on the ground beside him. In the sheltered work area, he loaded the brick grill with small chunks of wood for the fire.

Young Richard grabbed a bucket filled with blocks of hickory wood soaking in water. "Cook said you use these."

"Thanks. Do you know why?"

His blond curls swung with the swift movement of his head going up and down. "It's smelly wood."

Ellis chuckled. "Yes, you could say that. This hickory gives the food a great outdoors cooking taste." Ellis continued to pile the wood into the grill, then lit the kindling. Flames climbed the small pile.

Richard clapped his hands.

Ellis bowed. "Thank you." Richard stood proud, encircling his right arm around Ellis's left leg. A storm of emotions caught in Ellis's throat. How could a child love so easily, so unconditionally?

"Uncle Ellis?"

Ellis poked the burning embers with an iron rod and placed a couple of water-soaked hickory chunks on the pile.

"Yes, Richard?"

"How come Nanna couldn't race me to the corner?"

eight

"What?" Ellis's own voice echoed back at him off the shelter's tin roof. *Is that why she appeared so pale, so lethargic?*

Richard instantly released his clasp of Ellis's leg.

Ellis struggled to quell his uncharacteristic temper. "I'm sorry, I didn't mean to bellow. But I want to know what happened."

"Nanna doesn't yell," Richard whined.

"Son. . ." How could he explain this? It wasn't normal for him to yell either. He loved Richard and he was happy—no, honored to raise his brother's son. However, something—or rather someone—was getting the better of him. The constant fighting with himself not to think of a certain hazel-eyed nanny was wearing him down.

Ellis took a deep breath and went down to one knee, capturing the small boy's upper arms in his hands. "Normally, I don't yell either. I didn't mean to be so loud. Maybe I'm not used to having a lot of folks around me when I'm at home. Be patient with me, Son. I promise to try and not yell so often."

Richard scrunched his eyebrows together. "All right, Uncle Ellis. Nanna said some folks yell."

"Well, normally I don't. But I will try to be more careful. Deal?"

"Deal." Ellis held his hand out and Richard slipped his tiny hand into his. Such a good boy. A bright boy. And that was due to his nanny. His brother, if truth be told, had little to do with the raising of his own son.

"So tell me, why was Nanna racing you?"

"I asked her to."

"I see," he responded, carefully modulating his tone of

voice. He could see the boy felt terribly guilty. "Then what happened, Richard?"

"I won. But Nanna didn't feel so good. We stopped at Mrs. Vivian's house. She gave me cookies. Nanna sat and had some lemonade."

So, Miss Smith overexerted herself. Hadn't the doctor given her firm orders to stay down, relax? Not only did she not stay down, she actually raced the child. And what's a woman doing racing a small boy down the street anyway? Ellis fought to keep his resurgent anger from surfacing again. "Richard, I think your Nanna needs to rest some more."

"I know. Nanna said we can't go shopping or exploring."

"Right, not for a while."

"Nanna said she may never be able to."

What nonsense is this woman feeding the child? "I'm sure you'll be able to, real soon."

"Nanna said when she gets better, she'd be going home to New York."

So the woman doesn't want to stay in the area. Well no sense asking her to stay on. He'd just have to find a nanny somewhere on the island. Until then, he would have to alter his work schedule, take the lad to work with him whenever possible. Take him fishing on the dock even. Yup, he'd better start doing what he needed to do to take care of his nephew. It was apparent Miss Smith was breaking her ties with Richard and would be traveling home on the next ship.

The back of Ellis's neck tightened from the tension. He would do what was necessary for Richard. He didn't regret that. But the boy loved and depended on Miss Smith in more ways than she obviously knew. Here she was ready to release Richard into his care with barely a moment's thought. Maybe Beatrice Smith wasn't the kind of person he had been building her to be in his mind. Maybe raising Richard had just been a matter of duty, of patronage to an old friend.

Ellis massaged the back of his neck with his right hand and

sighed. *Guess it was good I hadn't offered her a permanent position as Richard's nanny, he told himself.*

❧

If looks could kill. . .

Beatrice swallowed hard and broke her gaze from Ellis's, who stood just outside the shelter glaring at her. What was he thinking? Those bluish-gray eyes of his, so dark beneath a deeply furrowed brow, bore into her. She had heard his outburst. Richard must have told him about their excursion.

"Excuse me, Cook. I believe I need to lie down. I don't think I'm up for dinner tonight."

"Nonsense, child. You need to eat." Cook crossed her hefty arms across her rounded stomach.

Beatrice lifted herself up off the chair. "Perhaps Richard could bring a little something later." She closed her eyes and rubbed her temples for emphasis. "I feel a headache coming on."

"Uh-huh." Cook eyed her cautiously.

"I just need to lie down. I'll be fine." She didn't want to overemphasize her physical weakness. Truth was, a tension-filled headache was coming on, but more out of fear of dealing with Ellis Southard, who already thought her a coddling nanny. Now he was certain to think her a fool as well. Why on earth had she agreed to race Richard today anyway?

"Mr. Ellis, he cooks a great steak. Can't say I enjoy anything else the man puts his hand to, food-wise that is. But outside on the grill—umm-hmm, the man can cook."

"I'm quite certain he can, but I really must go lie down now."

"Sure, you go run along now. Just remember to stop running sometime."

Bea squinted hard at Cook. Was she implying something here? Sure, she was old enough not to be running down a street after a child like that, but. . .did she mean something else? Beatrice turned and headed toward her cottage. Whatever the old woman meant, she wasn't going to wait around to find out. She'd seen enough of Cook to know she was able to read her thoughts. A wise woman, her father would have said. A nosy one, her Aunt Tilly would have said. In either case, Bea wasn't about to stick around to confirm Cook's suspicions that she might be running from Ellis Southard.

She opened the screen door and entered her cottage, letting the door slam behind her. It wasn't quite as cool as being outdoors under the banyan tree, but it was far cooler than earlier this afternoon. *Thank You, Lord, for this cool breeze tonight,* Bea silently prayed as she headed to the quiet sanctuary of her room.

Her bed, still rumpled from an earlier nap after her failed excursion with Richard, lay convictingly before her. Never would she have left a bed in that state back home.

Bea sighed and worked the wrinkles out of the bedding before collapsing on the rocker beside the bed. "Oh Lord, how long before I return home? I thought I would be happy with a few extra days with Richard. Instead I've gotten sick and I am miserable, Lord. I tried, Father, today I really tried to explain to him why I had to go home. I believe he understood. But I saw the pain in his eyes. Or was it fear, Father God? Please be with Richard; give him strength and bless his relationship with his uncle. Make it strong; give him the father he's never had. Amen."

Bea wiped tears off her cheeks with a delicate hand-laced handkerchief Elizabeth had made for her years ago. Embroidered on one corner were small purple violets, Bea's favorite flower. Bea sighed. "I've been a good mother to the child, just like you asked, Lizzy. But it hurts so much to let him go. I understand now why you held on so long, just one more day, one more hour to touch, to love that precious little boy. I grieve to be parting with him, but I know it is right, and I can't possibly live in this area with his uncle. I don't know if you ever met the man, Lizzy, but he is quite different from your Richard. Sometimes he terrifies me."

Bea stopped, realizing she'd been rambling aloud. It gave

her some relief to think her dear friend was looking down from heaven, yet she knew that only God could answer her pain, that only He could give peace to the heart-wrenching grief she was going through. She needed to return home. She needed to return soon. Why wait until she was recovered? The ship would be sailing into colder climate. Wouldn't that be better for her?

She lifted herself from the rocker, went to her garment bag, and pulled out a sheet of stationery. At the small desk in the farthest corner of the room she penned a letter to Mr. Ellis Southard.

❧

"Are they done yet?" Richard asked for the third time.

"Just about, Son. Why don't you go tell Nanna her steak is ready?"

"All right." Richard ran off toward the cottage. Ellis had seen her leave, wondered if she was all right, but figured Cook would have alerted him to any problem.

It was odd how old Cook sat relaxed in the chair with her feet up. Eyeing her from a distance, he realized she was slowing down. Not that he'd ever say anything to her about it. But he would like to see her do less walking and live with him. Her family could manage just fine without her. Probably should, too. The woman gave far too much to folks. She needed to slow down. Relax. Enjoy. . .

"Uncle Ellis!" Richard yelled.

Ellis smiled. At least outside it wasn't quite as piercing as in the house. He looked in the boy's direction but didn't answer.

"Nanna says she's not feeling up to dinner."

"Not up to dinner?" he mumbled.

"Cook?" He called as he brought the plates piled with mouth-watering steaks to the small table at her side.

"She said she needed to rest."

"Do you think she's all right?"

"I believe so. Think it's more her pride than heat."

"Ahh." Ellis would let that issue alone. He wasn't going to be baited by Cook into doing something he shouldn't. Like offering her the opportunity to stay on as Richard's nanny.

A quiet meal was eaten. Ellis grinned, reflecting. His father often said a quiet table meant the meal was exquisite. A small dinner plate was prepared for Miss Smith. Cook cleaned up, Richard delivered the meal, and Ellis retreated to his study.

The old wood floorboards shined from Cook's excellent housekeeping. She once told him it didn't need much fussin' 'cause he mostly sat in his chair at the desk. That had been true enough, but he'd begun pacing in recent days. Pacing and bellowing. "What a combination," he groaned.

"Uncle Ellis?"

A somber child stood in front of him.

"Yes, Richard."

"Nanna said to give you this."

Ellis reached for the thin piece of paper crumpled between the boy's chubby fingers. "Thank you, Son."

Not wanting to open the letter and be distracted from his nephew, he placed it in his trousers pocket. Whatever Miss Smith had to say could wait. The time before Richard went to bed was their private time, and Ellis cherished it.

"Would you like me to read a story for you tonight?" Ellis asked, combing the blond curls from Richard's face.

Richard beamed. "Can we play checkers?"

"Checkers it is. You get the pieces, I'll clear the table."

Richard scurried off.

Ellis lifted some papers he had brought home from his office and placed them on his desk.

"Good night, Mr. Ellis. Remember, I'll be comin' after breakfast tomorrow."

How could he forget? But he had. "Thanks for the reminder."

"You might ask Miss Smith to fix the morning meal," Cook suggested.

"I'll manage." After all, he would have to once Beatrice Smith moved back home. Until he found a suitable nanny or nurse, he would need to fend for himself and Richard.

"Oh, and one more thing, Mr. Ellis. I think the nanny is feeling somewhat useless," she added, tilting her head toward the cottage.

"Useless? What are you talking about, Cook?"

"I don't rightly know, but something is wrong with the dear gal. And I'm certain it isn't the heat."

Ellis snorted. "You call running wise?"

"That's nothing. I mean, yes, she shouldn't have pushed herself that way. But, well. . .I can't put my finger on it. But I knows something else is wandering around in that pretty little head."

Ellis shifted uneasily from one foot to the other. "She told Richard she was going home today."

"Mercy, no." Cook placed a hand over her heart.

"Afraid so. I'll talk with you tomorrow about this. Right now I don't want Richard hearing us."

"I can't figure what's going on. I knows she wants to be here with the child," Cook mumbled as she left the room.

Had Ellis heard her right? Beatrice Smith wants to be here? But why would she tell Richard. . .? Ellis dropped his hand into his pocket that held her letter.

" 'Bye, Cook," Richard called out. Ellis heard the pattering of his shoes on the hardwood floors and released the letter back into his pocket.

"I got it, Uncle Ellis."

"Excellent." Ellis rubbed his hands together. "Tonight I'm certain I'm going to win."

"I don't think so," Richard giggled. "You're worse than Nanna."

Ellis chuckled. Guess he needs to work on his losing skills some. "I wouldn't be too confident there. I was practicing today."

"You were?"

"Yup, an old sea captain showed me some pointers."

Richard's eyes widened. When was the time to start winning, Ellis wondered, in order to challenge the child more?

There was so much he still needed to learn about raising a boy.

Oh Lord, he said inwardly, *help me to know what's best.*

Ellis placed a white ivory checker in one hand and a black ivory checker in the other. He'd received the game as a gift from an old sailor who had carved it from whales' teeth. The board was of finely polished wood, with the black squares painted on. He put his hands behind his back, placing both checkers in his right hand. "Pick one."

Richard tapped his left arm. Ellis swung it around revealing his empty hand. Richard tapped the other and Ellis swung it around, after dropping the checkers in a back pocket and revealed it was empty also.

"Hey!" Richard placed his hands on his hips. "That's not how you do it, Uncle Ellis."

"It's not?" he asked, feigning innocence. Ellis scratched his head. "I know I put them in my hand. . ."

Richard chuckled. "Where are they?"

"I don't know." Ellis winked.

"Yes you do, you're trying to trick me."

"Am I? I know I put them in my hands; you saw me." Ellis turned around for affect and pretended to look for the missing checkers. Soon Richard was beside him searching.

"Where are they?" Richard asked.

"I don't know."

"Uncle Ellis, you're trying to trick me," Richard accused, his laughter growing louder by the moment.

Ellis roared in full-belly laughter, lunging across the table to tickle the boy.

❧

Laughter floated on the evening wind through Bea's cottage window, as it had every previous night. How could such a joyous sound be so heart-wrenching? How come she wasn't happy with the joy Richard had found with his uncle? How could she be so jealous? So self-centered? Bea wept into her pillow. "Father, God, I'm so terribly selfish."

nine

Ellis sat on the edge of his bed, the room dark, the house quiet. The gentle glow of candlelight beckoned his attention to the cottage below where Bea still placed the candle in her window for the boy. Ellis grinned briefly before pursing his lips in reflection. How could she truly love the child if she was so anxious to leave? Remembering the note, he reached into his pocket and pulled out what she had penned for him earlier.

Ellis lit the flame of his oil lamp beside the bed. The onion skin paper crinkled as he unfolded it. His eyes focused on the words flowing across the page in exquisite penmanship.

Dear Mr. Southard,

Would you be so kind as to procure my departure as soon as possible? I feel the trip home would do no further harm to my health in as much as Key West's climate is not agreeable at all.

I love Richard dearly, and ask only to be able to correspond with him. I hope you will find that acceptable. In time, I imagine Richard will have only vague memories of me. But I suppose that is how it should be.

Sincerely,
Beatrice Smith

Ellis's hand trembled. She did love the child, there was no question. But why couldn't she wait and give her body a chance to adjust to this area? *Why is she in such a hurry to return home, Lord? I don't understand.*

A whispered thought flickered past his ears. "Perhaps you should ask."

Should he? The hour was late. Was it proper to call on someone this late? To call on a single woman?

But she isn't just a single woman. She is the child's nanny. *And this is a matter that concerns the child,* he argued with himself. Didn't he, as Richard's guardian have the right to ask his nanny questions, no matter what the hour? Was there some law that forbade such things? He couldn't think of one.

Ellis turned down the lamp and headed out of his room. He straightened his shirt, removed some of the creases from his trousers, and headed down the stairs toward the front door, stopping to listen for Richard. He was sound asleep. He could leave him for a moment, he decided. Besides, the boy's bedroom window was open, and he was confident he could hear the child from the cottage.

A few long strides and he was at her door. He raised his hand to knock.

Then he lowered it.

He raised his hand again, but stopped short of tapping on the doorjamb.

He stepped back. Perhaps this should wait until morning.

He stood there undecided. Perhaps not. He stepped forward again.

Ellis muttered under his breath and rapped on the door. It protested in its frame, and instantly he regretted having knocked so hard.

"Hello?" a weak voice called from the bedroom.

"Miss Smith, I'm sorry to call on you so late. May I have a word with you?" *A bit formal, perhaps, but it got the point across,* he told himself.

"Mr. Southard, did you receive my letter?" she asked, peering around her partially opened door.

She had taken her hair down for the evening, its silken strands cascading over her shoulders. Ellis swallowed and cleared his throat. "Yes. Can we talk?"

"All right."

Her chocolate curls enhanced her delicate features. Ellis caught himself sniffing her hair as he followed her into the living room. Perhaps it was a mistake to have come in the evening. His palms beaded with sweat. He rubbed them dry with his fingers, only to find they immediately started to perspire again. He sat in the single chair in the living room, leaving her the sofa.

"Is there a reason you need to return home so quickly?" he asked. *Remain on the subject. . .you can get yourself through this.*

"No, nothing of a prcssing nature."

"Then why can't you remain a little longer? You should be feeling much better soon. Running was definitely not a wise undertaking, but it presents only a momentary setback."

"Is there a problem with procuring my return voyage?"

"No. I. . .I. . ."

❧

Beatrice searched his blue-gray eyes. He seemed strangely vulnerable, and yet so formal.

"Richard. . ."

"Is something wrong with Richard?" Bea jumped up from the sofa.

"I'm sorry. No, he's fine. I'm just concerned that your immediate departure would be terribly hard on the child."

"I spoke with him this afternoon. He seemed to understand my need to return home."

"Understand, yes. But is he ready to break his emotional connection with you?"

"I don't believe I've coddled the child as much as you think."

"Coddled? What are you talking about?"

"Coddling. The first day we met, you said I coddled the child."

Ellis stood up and approached her. "I may have said that, but I've come to see you have not coddled the boy at all. I've never met a woman who could bait a hook. And to hear

Richard say it, you're the best there is." Ellis winked.

Beatrice lowered her gaze and nervously rubbed her fingertips. "It took some practice."

"I can imagine. All the girls back home would scream and run away from me. Of course, I was threatening them with a fierce and mighty 'worm.' "

Bea giggled. "I can see Richard doing that one day."

Ellis chuckled. "Boys—we are different."

She sighed and relaxed. "I truly love him, and will miss him greatly, but my time in his life has come to an end."

"That may be, Miss Smith, but don't you see—a few more days or weeks won't hurt you, and those same days will help him tremendously."

"Perhaps. I just don't know how long I can survive in this heat."

"You're looking much better, and doing better. Granted, your little morning escapade was a supreme act of foolishness."

This man is some charmer. "Thanks."

"I'm sorry, I'm not your father. I have no right scolding you. But you do see the foolishness, don't you?"

"Of course I do. I saw it when I nearly passed out on Front Street. I thought I could handle the short distance. Richard and I did a lot of racing back home."

Ellis bobbed his head.

"I suppose you think a lady shouldn't do such things."

"Now don't go putting words into my mouth, Miss Smith." Ellis shook a finger in the air. "I've never seen a woman running before, that's all."

"I reckon. But you grew up on Richard's family farmstead. You know there are no children around for miles. The boy needed a playmate, as well as a mother, father, nurse, teacher, and whatever else needed doing at the time."

"True. I always had my brother Richard to play with. Granted, he was older, but it was still someone."

Bea sat back down on the sofa and Richard returned to his chair.

"Miss Smith, please tell me you'll stay for a few more days, perhaps a week or so."

"I would love to explore this island some. I've been trapped in this yard for days, and while you do have a charming yard and beautiful garden, I would like to see more."

Ellis grinned. "I understand. But. . ."

Bea watched his hesitancy, his hands folding and unfolding. "I need you to be spending your free time with the boy. I don't think courting would be proper."

"Courting? What on earth are you talking about?" She watched his eyes focus on his lap. Was he considering asking her to court him? Couldn't be, he'd hardly even looked at her since her arrival.

"Sorry. I had a gentleman caller today who asked for my permission to seek the pleasure of your company."

"He asked you?" She huffed. How dare the man. She wasn't Ellis Southard's ward. She wasn't anyone's ward. She had a free mind and a bright one at that, and she would determine whom she would or would not court.

"Now before you get yourself worked into a tizzy, let me explain that Mr. Dabny comes from the North. Where, as you probably know, in good society a man comes to the father before approaching the woman."

How could she possibly forget? She was born and bred in that society, and while Ellis Southard didn't have an inkling of her true social status, she shouldn't have been so offended.

"I see," she said, her voice controlled.

"I let Marc know he would have to ask you himself."

Well that ended any lingering doubt she might have had that Ellis's intentions were to court her. No, while she had noticed how handsome Ellis was, obviously he didn't have any attraction toward her. On the other hand, hadn't she caught him staring at her when she first greeted him at the door?

Ellis appeared to be awaiting her answer. What was his question. . .?

"Thank you."

"You're welcome." Ellis shifted in his chair and pulled at his collar with his right forefinger. "Do you agree you shouldn't be socializing?"

"Mr. Southard, whether I do or do not accept Mr. Dabny's offer has little or nothing to do with my care of Richard. Wouldn't you agree that once you are home for the evening, my time is my own?"

Ellis squirmed. "I reckon."

Bea smiled. "Then if I should accept an invitation from Mr. Dabny or anyone else, it would be when my duties as Richard's nanny are over for the day."

She couldn't believe her own ears. Was she really telling this man she was going to get on with her life, begin socializing again? Allow for the possibility of a courtship? A prickly feeling climbed her spine.

"Very well, Miss Smith." Ellis lifted himself from the chair.

She'd done it again. The man became an instant board around her. Straight, rigid, and totally unfeeling. "Why do you do that?"

"Do what?"

"Put up a wall of defense around me. Just when I think we are beginning to talk like normal people, you pull back into. . . into. . .a plank. Stiff, unbending, un—"

Fire ignited in Ellis's eyes. He closed them, and when he lifted his lids again his eyes were stone cold, dark, and piercing. "Good night, Miss Smith."

For a moment she thought she had reached him. But it was gone in a flash. With long strides to her door he made a hasty retreat. If the man had any appreciation for her as a woman, he sure kept it well hidden. No, she could never stay in Key West. Living under the same roof with a man she found so attractive she lost sleep over, yet who seemed almost repulsed by her, would be nerve-racking to say the least. Still, he wasn't truly heartless. He had spoken words of appreciation for the fact that she would even bait a hook for the sake of his nephew. "I'm so confused," she huffed.

❧

Ellis stomped back up to the house. How could she be so casual about courting? And why did he feel like a child caught with his hand in the cookie jar? Fact was, he would like to explore the option of courting the woman, but he was too afraid of himself, of his responses, of her beauty.

Ellis groaned. "Heather, I'm so sorry." His past, his mistake, would continue to haunt him when in the presence of someone as tempting as Beatrice Smith. Her beauty was only part of the attraction. Her strong, determined spirit. Her ability to reason. Her way with Richard. These traits and so many more formed the foundation of his attraction. An attraction he could never act upon.

No, he was not a man to be trusted.

ten

Beatrice saw nothing of Ellis Southard the following day. He even missed his evening meal with the family. "Is he still angry, Lord? And what is he so angry about, anyway?" she rambled in prayer, pacing the small cottage floor from the front room into her bedroom. "I only agreed it was my business if and when I accepted anyone's invitation."

Marc Dabny had been a perfect gentleman, but she had turned him down. For a moment she considered accepting his invitation just to get a rise out of Ellis Southard. But she saw the intensity of Mr. Dabny's interest as a wife-hunter, and she would not be the woman to break the man's heart. Better to leave a man before he's attached, she felt. Not to mention his intentions were totally self-motivated and had little to do with "love."

Given Ellis's recent behavior, all signs seemed to indicate that he was avoiding her. She'd never been so offensive to another individual and that bothered her. Of course, the other side of this meant that, by his absence, she wouldn't be led down the wrong path of temptation.

To Ellis's credit, he did manage to make time for Richard that evening. As she stayed within the confines of her cottage, laughter drifted across the yard once again, creating within her a longing to be in the middle of such joyous activity.

The candle on the windowsill remained unlit, as per young Richard's instructions. He had proclaimed during dinner that he was a big boy now and didn't need it. The unlit candle was now a solemn, cold reminder of her time to release Richard and give him to his uncle and new life.

"Nanna!" she heard Richard call. Bea raced to the window which faced Richard's room, lifted the screen in its wooden track, and waved. A wide smile filled his face, his small arms wiggling back and forth. Bea could see Ellis's strong arm wrapped around Richard's small waist. A proud smile softened Ellis's otherwise rigid stance.

"Good night, Nanna. I love you."

"Good night, Richard. I love you, too." With all the energy she could muster, she stepped back from the window and lowered the screen. Mosquitoes thrived on this island, in numbers she'd never seen before. Grateful for the mosquito netting draped around her bed, she checked its corners again to make certain it hung properly, then prepared for bed.

Sitting in front of the vanity, Bea let down her hair. As a child she had worn it loose. After her coming-out party she had taken to wearing it up in public, wrapped into a tight bun and generally hidden beneath a hat or scarf, in keeping with proper etiquette. A nightly custom of a hundred strokes kept her thick curls from snarling in her sleep. She loved the feel of her hair on her shoulders and back, sometimes feeling a little ashamed of her own vanity. She'd known many women who would curse their hair, wearing it in all kinds of unnatural styles, and fuss and fume when it didn't do what they wanted.

Her hair brushed, she sat down to read before retiring for the night. Lost in her loneliness, the comfort of her nightly ritual had a hollow feel.

❧

"Uncle Ellis?" Richard looked up from his pillow.

"Yes, Richard." Ellis sat down on the edge of Richard's bed.

"Is Nanna going to always sleep over there?"

How could he tell the boy she would be leaving soon? Granted, Miss Smith had prepared him for her departure, but. . .

"No."

"Can she move into the big house?"

"I don't think so, Son. She'll be going back to New York."

"Will you be going to New York too?"

Ugh, Ellis inwardly groaned. For a child he sure did ask difficult questions. "Richard, it's late, and you need to get your sleep. Remember, we're going fishing in the morning."

Richard nodded his head and wiggled himself under the covers.

"Is Nanna coming fishing?"

"No, Son. Not tomorrow."

"When?" Richard lifted his head up off the pillow.

"I don't know. When she's well enough. Now, let's say your prayers."

"Yes, sir." Richard laid back down and clasped his tiny fingers together. "Dear Jesus, tell Mommy and Daddy I miss them. Help Nanna be happy again. And bless Uncle Ellis and Cook. Amen."

"Amen," Ellis echoed.

Help Nanna be happy again? *Was she upset with the boy?* he wondered. Truth be told, he had avoided her today. Was she still upset regarding their conversation last night? Did she regret her decision to postpone her departure even for a few days?

Ellis kissed Richard on the forehead. "Good night, Richard."

"Good night, Uncle Ellis."

Ellis closed the door to the child's room and headed down the stairs to his study. Invoices needed posting. Jedidiah Brighton had managed to load additional sponges to carry to New York. Pleased with the sales and the plentiful supply of natural sponges on the various reefs around the small island, his business would continue to grow. The Bahamian men he hired were naturals in the water and excellent sponge fishermen.

A parrot cawed, and Ellis looked out the window. The sky, a blanket of dark velvet with a silver pearl nestled on it, created a wonderful backdrop for his tropical garden. He lowered his glance to the cabin in his backyard. Scratching his beard, he wondered if it was wrong to separate the nanny from the boy. Should he offer her a permanent position to stay in Key West? He had assumed from the start she would want to get back to her life in New York. From their conversation last night, he finally understood that Richard was her life. She had poured her heart and soul into the child. And his brother had spoken highly of her competency. Maybe he should ask her to stay in charge of the boy's care.

Ellis leaned his chair back on its two hind legs and plopped his feet on his desk, a bad habit he never saw the need to break. Maybe he should pray about this. He'd been praying about how to be a good father to Richard, and reading every verse in Scripture he could find about children and disciplining them. But had he actually asked God if Miss Smith should remain on for a time as his nephew's nanny? Or was he simply allowing her to leave because of his attraction to her, not wanting to fight with temptation? Not wanting to deal with his past, his. . .

Yes, prayer was most definitely in order.

❧

The next morning, Bea woke early and hurriedly dressed. She knew of Ellis's and Richard's fishing plans. She'd hoped for an invitation. Oddly enough, she'd gotten used to the sport. She'd done it simply to do "manly" things with Richard, and much to her surprise found she actually enjoyed it. The peaceful ripple of the water allowed one to think and pray. She'd never fished in an ocean before. In fact, until she boarded the *Justice* in New York harbor to come to Key West, she'd never even seen an ocean. The vast water contrasted dramatically to the mountain springs that fed the various farms she'd lived on in upstate New York. The smell of salt permeated the air. Low tide. . .well, low tide left something to be desired.

The movement of the water was different as well. In the springs it flowed in one constant direction; the ocean flowed in different directions depending on the tides. And the gentle roll of the surf as it lapped the shore was just as captivating as the constant movement of the water rushing downstream. While she found the two types of water very different, they both had the same soothing effect on her—gratitude to her heavenly Father. It gave her something to remind her of home.

Late last evening she had penned a letter to her parents, hoping there would be a boat heading to New York so she could hand it to the captain. She tapped her pocket in her long apron-covered shirt to be certain it was still there. . . Perhaps the *Justice* would be coming back from Cuba soon, and she could send it that way.

The large front door opened and out stepped Richard with his pole in hand, immediately followed by Ellis Southard. Richard's bright smile filled his face. Ellis's eyes sparkled as he watched his nephew maneuver the fishing pole down the front steps.

Perhaps I shouldn't. . . Bea stepped forward from the trees' shadows. "Good morning, gentlemen."

"Nanna! Are you going fishing?" Richard ran up to her.

She glanced over to Ellis. His eyes no longer sparkled. He didn't want her along. "No, I have a letter I need to post."

Richard pouted. "Why don't you want to come fishing with me?"

I do, child, I really do, she wanted to say, but held back her emotions and her tongue.

"If you would like to come with us, Miss Smith," Ellis paused, "you are welcome."

"I would enjoy it, but I wouldn't want to intrude."

Ellis grinned and then sobered. "Come along then, and be quick about it."

Bea tucked the letter back into the apron over her skirt and placed her hands on her hips. "Ready when you are, sir."

"Yeah! Nanna's coming." Richard pranced up and down.

Looking over at Ellis Southard, she noticed he stiffened and shut down his emotions. Why did the man keep doing that? Bea rolled the tension out of her shoulders. She didn't understand him, but she would have to accept the discomfort of the day. After all, she had wormed herself a place in this little fishing expedition.

"Let's go."

Ellis bolted ahead and walked a brisk pace through the streets to the harbor and down one of the large wooden docks that reached far into the ocean. Lined with sponges, nets, and a variety of ropes in different widths and sizes, she surmised that the dock belonged to Ellis and his sponging company. Afraid to ask, she held her tongue.

She worked up a sweat just keeping pace with Ellis Southard. Even Richard seemed a bit tired from the walk. She slowed her pace. She wasn't going to fall victim to heat exertion again. Little Richard's legs took three steps for every one of Ellis's.

As Bea and Richard started walking on the wooden planks, Ellis stood at the end of the pier. He turned to face her, and muttered something to himself, muffled by the expansive ocean. Bea and Richard continued to plod on down the dock. Bea decided a word with Ellis Southard about his careless behavior was in order. But she would wait so that little Richard wouldn't be privy to their conversation.

Bea sat on the edge of the dock beside Richard and dangled her legs over the water. "It's a pleasant morning, Richard, don't you think?"

"Yup." Richard's head turned as he scanned the horizon. "Nanna, see those clouds?"

Bea looked to where he pointed and nodded.

"Uncle Ellis says they are spinning around like a top."

She looked over to the horizon. Half a dozen small funnel clouds stood up from the sea. "Really?"

"Yup. And you see those clouds over there?" Richard pointed straight in front of them.

Bea nodded again.

"Those are new clouds being made."

"Do you know how clouds are made?" Bea inquired.

"Yup, Uncle Ellis says the sun makes the water hot and it 'vaporates, and when it gets high in the sky, it turns white and becomes a cloud."

"I see." For a four year old he really had quite an acute mind. Pleased and impressed that Ellis could talk with Richard in a way he could understand, she decided to acknowledge those things when she confronted him.

❧

Beatrice Smith's presence this morning annoyed Ellis. She'd known he planned to take Richard fishing. And she obviously made herself available to come with them. Was he jealous of Richard's affection for her, or fighting his own attraction? He wasn't certain. Last night, in his stocking feet, he had buffed the floor to a high gloss from his continuous pacing. Successfully, he had resisted the urge to go to her cottage and speak to her, wanting, longing, to come up with any excuse just to see her smiling face.

Richard had thrived from Beatrice Smith's care. In his opinion, his brother had made a terrible error in judgment. How a man could avoid his own child because the mother died was beyond him. He understood his brother's deep love for his wife, but wasn't young Richard a part of her that continued to live?

Maybe he should let Beatrice and Richard return to the farm. But his brother's wishes were most emphatic that Ellis raise his son if anything should happen to him. And dealing with his own past would be at stake if he returned to New York, having been warned never to step foot again in the state, or Heather's father would press charges. He knew from Richard's letters that Heather had married. Perhaps enough time had passed.

"Nanna, Nanna, help!" Richard cried with excitement.

"Hold on tight, Richie."

Bea stood behind the boy, allowing him to work the fish and bring it in. Ellis smiled. Anxious to help, and yet proud to watch, he stationed himself beside the child.

Instinctively, they both reached for the line to help pull in the fish. Their hands grazed each other's, and Bea abruptly pulled hers away. Ellis held the line and pulled the fish up on the dock.

"It's blue and green!" proclaimed Richard.

"It's a snapper. Good eating, I think you'll like this fish," Ellis offered.

Richard jumped up and down around the fish. "Can I eat it for breakfast?"

Ellis placed his foot gently on the fish to keep it from flapping itself back into the water. "I imagine Cook would be happy to prepare it for you."

"Nanna can do it. Can't you, Nanna?"

Bea smiled and nodded her head.

"I'm sure she can, but Cook gets fussy about who she lets in her kitchen."

"Oh." Richard held Bea's hand. "Nanna, is it okay if Cook does it?"

"Yes, it's like Daisy in New York. She prefers to do all the cooking."

"Yeah, but not the fish. You had to clean the fish."

"I remember." Bea smiled. "That's a mighty fine catch, Richie."

She even cleans fish. Of course, if she wasn't too weak to put a worm on a hook, it only stood to reason she was capable of cleaning a fish, too. Even though Beatrice informed him she was the child's playmate, father, mother, nanny, etc., the other night, he realized he was just getting a glimmer of the real person. Beatrice Smith certainly was a unique woman. Aside from Cook, he had never met such a bold woman. But, Cook was another kind altogether.

"Can you remove the hook or should I?" Ellis asked.

"Nanna does that."

"Nanna." Ellis motioned her to take her place in the tradition of Richard's fishing. "Be aware of the spines on the dorsal fin."

Bea simply nodded and knelt on her skirt and gracefully

removed the hook from the fish. "Looks like you shall have a big breakfast this morning, Richard."

Richard beamed. His smile ran from one side of his face to the next. Ellis loved the boy. He would be staying with him whether in New York or here, it didn't matter.

❧

Bea placed the fish in the small bucket Ellis brought. The tropical fish flapped and fluttered, slapping the sides of the bucket with its tail.

"Can we go home now, Uncle Ellis?"

Ellis searched Bea's eyes for an answer to his silent, "Why?"

"Once Richard catches a fish, his only interest is his tummy," Bea chuckled.

Ellis smiled. "Sure, Son. I'm quite certain Cook will be happy to see your breakfast."

"Come on, Nanna. Let's get a head start on uncle Ellis," Richard called out as he started down the pier toward shore.

Bea turned and whispered to Ellis. "Sir, you might want to remember, small boys have small legs and can't keep the pace of a full-grown man."

Ellis nodded and went in the opposite direction to pick up his pole and tackle. Bea carried the bucket and Richard's pole. The boy was determined to beat his uncle Ellis home.

Ellis sidled up beside her, tenderly removing the bucket from her hand. "Thank you for your admonition. However, Richard will need to learn to take care of his pole and catch."

"Generally he does. I believe he wishes to show you how much of a man he really is."

"A man, huh? He needs to enjoy being a boy longer. There's plenty of time for being a man."

"Perhaps, but he's had more losses than most my age. He's had to grow up fast. All of this," Bea spanned the area around them with her outstretched hand, "is an adventure. Soon he will need to mourn the loss of his father, his home and. . .me."

eleven

Cook smothered Richard with praises for his fine catch and breakfast. After a simple fare of fresh poached eggs with toast, freshly squeezed orange juice, and Richard's catch of the day, Ellis slipped off to work with a single salutation.

If Bea wasn't careful, she would soon start daydreaming about Ellis. He was such an interesting character, with a kind and gentle side full of passion and warmth, as she'd witnessed in his interchanges with Richard. But there was this other darker side of him that held everyone at bay. His emotions seemed to run hot and cold. She had been too forward the other evening, addressing him on this part of his personality.

❧

"What be on your pretty mind, Miss Bea?" Cook inquired as she helped her out of her corset at the end of another long day.

"Nothing."

"I don't know what it is with you young folks, always carrying on and saying nothing is on your mind when it's obvious there is plenty happenin' up there."

"I'm sorry, I'm not used to sharing my personal thoughts."

"I reckon it should be me apologizing for prying where I shouldn't be. Some say I have a problem with that. On the other hand, I tend to believe it's my duty to get beyond the surface and sink right down to the heart of the matter. You wouldn't be thinking about when you leave Master Richard, would you now?"

"Truth be told, it has been on my mind. But no, that wasn't what I was pondering. How well do you know Mr. Southard?"

"I suppose I've known him longer than most. He wasn't much of a man when he landed on this here rock. At the time he come, let me think, I believe it was 1850 or '51—sometime thereabouts—there weren't too many folks living here. I heard say there was around a thousand. Personally I never had a mind to count 'em."

"He's been here that long?"

"Wet behind the ears and carrying a heap of trouble on his back. He never did say what he was running from, but he's made his peace with it. At least I think he has."

Bea's curiosity rose a notch. Why had he left New York? If she recalled correctly, he was seventeen at the time. In all her talks with Elizabeth she'd never really been curious as to why he left. It simply hadn't seemed all that important.

"He seems to have a good heart."

"I see, you're worried about him being a good man to raise the child."

Bea nodded.

"There's few men with as fine a moral character as Mr. Southard. He works hard, cares for those around him, treats people fairly. He'll do right by the boy."

Bea's heart tightened. Soon she would be leaving Richard. And oddly enough, he would go on and hardly remember her, and yet, he had profoundly affected her for the rest of her life. "Cook, do you know if the *Justice* has come back from Cuba?"

"Come and gone. Why do you ask?" Cook was folding her corset and placing it on the chair beside the chest of drawers.

"I thought perhaps I should seek transport back home."

"But Mr. Ellis hasn't hired a nanny yet."

"I know but. . ."

"Ahh, I understand, child. Your heart is breaking."

Gentle tears rolled out of her eyes. "Yes. It's so hard, Cook. I love Richard as if he were my own. But I have no rights to him. And Ellis is. . .well, he is his uncle." Bea sniffed and immediately she found herself engulfed in Cook's soft, loving arms.

"There, there, child. Trust the Good Lord; He knows what is best."

"I'm trying, and He's been trying to teach me Ecclesiastes 3:5, 'a time for embracing, and a time to refrain from embracing.' "

"Personally I don't know what Mr. Ellis's problem is with having you continue on as the child's nanny, but I reckon men don't have an eye for maternal love."

"Cook, I. . .well, I am not a normal nanny. I was Richard's mother's best friend. I come from high society. I gave it all up just to help my friend. And now I love Richard not because he is Elizabeth's son, but because he has become so dear to me. He's as close as the air I breathe."

"I'm not surprised about your status in society, but what does that matter? You love the child, the child loves you that should be the end of it."

"But it's not, and we both know Mr. Southard is not happy with me."

"Does he know? Your status, I mean."

"I can't imagine he does. I've not told him. Besides, I was eight when he left, and it's as you say, it doesn't matter."

"Maybe. If the man knew what you've given up for the child, perhaps he might think differently about you," Cook huffed. "I tell you, the man hasn't been right since you arrived. If I didn't know better, I'd think he fancies you."

"What? You can't be serious. He can barely stand to be in the same room with me."

"Precisely my point."

"Cook, you've been out in the sun too long. He can't possibly. . ." Bea couldn't even continue the thought. There was no way on God's green earth that Ellis Southard was attracted to her. However, if the tables were turned she would have to admit she was mighty attracted to him.

"Think what you will, child, you might be right. I'm just an old woman who's lived too long."

"Nonsense."

Cook smiled. "I must be leaving your wonderful company, Miss Bea. My family needs me. They just love to tell me how their days went and to hear about mine. I must tell you, you coming from New York has made for some delightful stories these many days."

"Oh my." Bea blushed.

Cook hugged her again. "Trust the Lord, child. He knows the desires of your heart."

Bea felt the heat on her cheeks deepen. God truly did know all her desires, which included the temptation that one Mr. Ellis Southard had caused since her arrival on Key West.

❧

Ellis's ears still rang from the chastisement Cook gave him for not allowing Beatrice Smith to stay on as Richard's nanny. She had a point. Several in fact. And he had considered the idea. He just didn't know if it was the wisest thing for him to do. He couldn't deny his attraction to her. Yet, he knew better than to act on such impulses. Could he possibly allow her to live in his home and not react to her presence? Ellis paced his office floor.

A dim light still burned in Bea's cottage. Bea's cottage? When had he given her possession of the place? Beatrice Smith was like that. Whatever she touched, wherever she went was illuminated by her presence. She was an incredible woman. But he was a man not to be trusted around women.

Key West had been a perfect place to settle. So few women, so few temptations. It was easy to get lost in his work here and avoid the fairer sex. As the years passed and more women moved to the island, he had remained in control. He'd even escorted a few of the ladies to church and social functions from time to time, and had become the perfect gentleman.

Ellis snickered. Heather O'Donald and her father would never believe that.

What if Bea remained in the cottage? He could remodel the place to suit her needs. She probably came from a home about that size before she became Richard's nanny. Ellis scratched his beard and gently stroked it back in place with long, thoughtful strokes. He peeked out the window. A single lamp glowed. If he was going to ask her to stay on, he'd better do it now before reason won over.

Ellis's steps were fluid and fast as he made his way out of the house to the captain's quarters cabin. Taking a deep breath, he lifted his hand and paused. Should he? He held his knuckles suspended in the air. Perhaps he should pray about this, consider all the ramifications of how this woman would bring him to the brink of his self-control.

He turned around and stepped away. Only to be halted by Cook's words. "What are you afraid of?"

What indeed? Cook didn't know. No one knew. Well, Heather O'Donald and her father did. But his brother, the only other person who knew, was gone. A gentle voice whispered in his head. "It's been fifteen years."

Ellis knocked the doorjamb with his knuckle.

"Who is it?" Bea asked behind the still closed door.

"Miss Smith, it is me, Ellis. May I have a word with you?"

Bea slowly opened the door.

Ellis took in a sharp breath. She was lovely. She looked like a young girl rather than a grown woman with her long brown hair curled in spirals, cascading over her shoulders and framing her lily white neck. He swallowed and cleared his throat to speak. He'd seen her with her hair down before, but now the stark difference in their ages was once again made apparent. "May I come in?"

"Yes." Bea stepped back and allowed him to enter.

Ellis began to pace.

"What's the matter, Mr. Southard? Is Richard okay?"

"He's fine. Sorry. I. . .well I. . .I wanted to ask you something."

"Please sit, you're making me nervous," Bea pleaded.

"Sorry." Richard sat on the sofa. Bea sat a respectable distance away from him.

"I don't know how to say this other than to state my business straight out. Do you have obligations in New York?"

"No. Not really. Why do you ask?"

"What do you mean 'not really'?"

She hesitated, took in a deep breath, then looked him

straight in his eyes. His heart stopped beating from the deep scrutiny he felt coming from her hazel-eyed gaze.

"My family wishes to have another coming-out party for me upon my return."

"Coming-out?"

"Mr. Southard, I come from a family such as your own. I took the job as Richard's nanny because of my deep love for Elizabeth. We all assumed she would get better shortly after she gave birth, but that simply wasn't the case. As you are well aware."

"You did all of that for the love of a friend?"

Bea nodded.

"I am in awe of you, Miss Smith. There are few who would sacrifice so much for the love of another."

"Thank you, but it hasn't been a sacrifice."

Ellis looked around the cottage. Such humble furnishings, and she was accustomed to the finer things in life, yet not once did she complain or voice her disapproval. Nor had she informed him who she was and his obligations to arrange proper housing for her stay.

"I am sorry, Miss Smith, if I had known. . ."

"Nonsense, I didn't need to tell you. I wanted to be with Richard, he's. . .he's special."

"He's more than special to you. You love him as if he were your own."

Bea looked away and whispered, "Yes."

"I came to ask you to stay on as his nanny, but I can't do that now. Knowing who you are, I can't ask you to give up your life again for Richard."

"I would love to stay on as Richard's nanny. Wealth isn't that important to me. Mind you, I'm not saying I don't appreciate some of the finer things. But Richard is of far more importance than wealth to me. I would be honored to stay on as his nanny."

"I can't allow you. It just wouldn't be right."

"Who is to know? If I don't care, why should you?" Bea

reached over and touched his arm. "Ellis, please let me stay."

Bea was trembling from her contact with Ellis. "I've prayed, I've asked God for a way for me to continue to be a part of Richard's life. In six years, he will be ten and I will still be young enough to marry."

"Beatrice. . .Bea. . .I, I just wouldn't feel right. You should be marrying a man and raising your own children."

"I don't want that as much as I want to be with Richard. Can't you understand? I love him that much." Bea swallowed back the tears that threatened to fall.

Ellis took her hand from his arm and held it tenderly within his own callused palm, massaging the tops of her fingers with the ball of his thumb. He glanced into her eyes and raised her chin with his left forefinger.

Bea's heart hammered in her chest. She was drawn to this man in a way she couldn't put into words.

Ellis touched the ringlets of her hair. "You're an incredibly beautiful woman, Bea."

Bea blushed. His eyes filled with passion. The realization excited her and frightened her at the same time. She removed her hand from his and rose from the sofa.

Ellis followed and stood behind her. "I'm sorry for being so forward, Beatrice. Please forgive me."

Bea nodded. She didn't trust herself to speak.

He placed his hands on her shoulders. "I would like to get to know you. May I call again tomorrow evening? After Richard is in bed."

"Yes," she whispered, her voice shaky, her body protesting. A driving need to turn to him and bury herself into his embrace threatened any sense of decency and proper behavior she had ever been taught.

He stepped back and removed his hands from her shoulders. As if instantly chilled, she shivered. What was the matter with her?

She turned to the gentle click of her door being shut. He was gone now. The cottage seemed darker. Lonelier. A somber air filled the empty space.

Oh Lord, what has come over me? Over us? She truly would have to admit Ellis's eyes spoke of his untold desire. She wondered if her own eyes revealed the same passion.

twelve

All the next day, Ellis found himself as edgy as a land crab in search of shelter and protection. He had almost lost his self-control last night. He prayed long into the night, thanking the Lord for stepping in and pulling them apart at the moment He had. Granted, Bea had possessed the wisdom and strength to break the connection that drew them to each other. Bea had found the resolve to step away from him and their passion. And yes, she had the same desires as he.

What was it about him and his desires which brought a woman to a point of forgetting all propriety? He must be some kind of beast or animal, unable to control his desires.

On the other hand, they needed to talk. A physical attraction between them could not be denied. But could they live so close to one another and not succumb to temptation? Ellis was quite certain he would not stand the test. He hadn't in the past. What gave him a chance of withstanding it in the present? Especially since his desires for Beatrice far outweighed any desires he ever had for Heather.

Cook was exceptionally cold to him this morning. He didn't have the strength to tell her he had gone to ask Bea to stay on, only to find out that he couldn't allow her to take the position due to her social standing.

He felt grateful his parents were no longer alive. They would not be shamed once again by his actions. They had never known exactly what he had done, but they understood from Richard, Ellis had no choice but to leave, for the family's honor.

"Honor," Ellis sighed. "Father, God, why did You do this to me? Why bring a woman into my path that I can never have? If we should ever marry, she would be a social outcast for marrying the likes of me. It wouldn't be fair to her, Lord. I couldn't put her through that."

"Through what?" Bea asked.

"Bea." Ellis fought every muscle in his body to stay in place. "Miss Smith, I was unaware of your presence."

"Apparently, and you do that quite well. How long have you been practicing the cold, standoffish man?"

"Long enough."

"Ellis, something happened between us last night. Don't you think we ought to talk about it?"

Ellis turned and faced the window looking over the gardens. "I was forward last evening, Miss Smith. It will never happen again."

"Oh, so if I came over to you right now and placed my fingers upon your chest, you would not respond?"

"Don't!"

"Don't what, Ellis? Admit that I'm attracted to you?" He heard the shuffle of her dress behind him.

"Yes. . .no. Bea, we can't."

"We can't, or you won't?" She placed her hand upon his left shoulder.

"I won't."

"Why?" she whispered.

"I am not an honorable man." Ellis walked away from her grasp.

"What?" Confusion knitted the features of her pretty face.

The sun was setting and the pinks and purples of the sunlight set a rose-colored haze across the garden.

"I have a past I'm ashamed of, Bea. I can never return to New York."

❧

Never return to New York? What kind of crime had he committed? Is that why he left town and never returned so many years before?

"Fine. Be that way. I can't force you to explain. However, I think you're afraid. I certainly am. What we saw in each other's eyes last night was. . .was. . .well, I don't know what it was. But I know one thing, it scared the life out of me."

Bea retreated from Ellis's study. It had been a forward move to approach him in the house rather than to wait for him to come to her cottage later. But it seemed safer to speak with him there, while Cook was still in the house and with Richard running around.

She found Richard playing in his room. She now knew she couldn't stay, even if Ellis offered her the position. Whatever was going on between the two of them was unstoppable if she remained. And Bea wasn't all that certain she wanted to find out what it was. She had been known to speak her mind occasionally, but she prided herself on her ability to remain in control. Last night, she was not in control. And neither was Ellis. If they had kissed at that moment it would have been. . . Bea shook the thought right out of her mind. She would not allow herself to ponder such things again.

All night she had tossed and turned, hoping that she and Ellis might have a future together. And that, through their union, the three of them would become a family. And Richard would legally become her son. *Such foolish thoughts,* she chided herself. Ellis had no intentions of giving into his feelings. Instead he erected a stone wall around himself that she was too afraid to climb.

"Richie."

"Yes, Nanna."

"I want you to know I love you very much." She fought for control of her emotions and continued. "I will always love you."

"I love you too, Nanna."

She balled her hands into fists and released them, working out her tension. "Like I mentioned the other day, I'm going home, Richie."

"Home? To my New York house?"

"No, to my parents' New York house. You remember visiting my parents' house, don't you?"

"Yes. But Nanna, I want you to stay."

"I'd love to, but I can't. Your uncle Ellis loves you very much, and he will take good care of you. Perhaps when you are older and a man yourself you could come for a visit and see me in New York."

"I'll visit you, Nanna." Richard grabbed her legs through the loose-fitting Spanish-style skirt she had purchased the other day.

Bea pulled him up in her arms and hugged him hard, groaning and giving him a great big bear hug. "I don't know exactly when I'll be leaving. I have to wait for a ship. Hopefully, I'll have a few days to spend with you before I go."

"Can we go fishing?"

She grasped him more firmly. His bright blue-gray eyes darted back and forth imploring her to say yes. How could she not? "Sure, how about tomorrow morning?"

"Yippee."

Bea smiled. A child could shift his or her emotions as easily as the wind. One minute, sad about her leaving. The next, excited to go fishing. She set him back down on the floor. "I'll see you tomorrow morning. Good night, Richie."

" 'Night, Nanna." Richie continued to play with his blocks on the floor, his face intense as he worked on his next masterpiece.

Bea slipped into the hallway and tentatively approached the staircase. This was now the second time she broached the subject of her leaving to Richard, and it was getting easier, for him and for her. Perhaps she would be able to get over the tremendous loss in time.

At the foot of the stairs the darkened silhouette of Ellis Southard stood, waiting, his stance rigid, even more than before, if that were possible. Bea took in a deep breath and descended the stairs. "Good evening, Mr. Southard."

❧

How could she be so casual? Ellis reached out to her and pulled her toward him. Fear blazed in her eyes. He paused, then released her. "Good night, Miss Smith."

The stunned woman stood in front of him. He stepped back. Timidly she reached her hand toward his forearm, but before it connected she pulled it back.

"I'm taking Richard fishing in the morning. Then I'll begin searching for a ship to make my departure. I think it would be best."

Ellis didn't want her to leave, but he didn't trust himself around her. The temptation he had felt with Heather was nothing compared to the pull of this woman. Unable to speak, he simply nodded his assent.

She turned and walked out the front door. She would be out of his life soon. The temptation would be gone. He could get back to living his quiet life. Ellis eased out a pent-up breath.

"Uncle Ellis," Richard hollered from up the stairs. Perhaps his life wouldn't be all that quiet. He mounted the stairs two at a time and hurried to the child.

❧

Bea set out for town after cleaning up from her morning fishing expedition with Richard. Unlike the time before, Ellis had not joined them. There must be a ship going to New York. She fortified her resolve to go back home.

Most ships passed through the Key West seaport as they worked their way from the states to the Caribbean or vice versa. Disappointed to find all the ships sailing in the wrong direction, Bea headed toward a small shop she had passed earlier. Purchasing some gifts for her family might help her to focus on New York rather than on what she was leaving behind. A few more days on Key West would give her a few more days with Richard. Granted, the tension between Ellis and herself would probably mount, but. . .

Bea's heart caught in her chest. She saw Ellis working on his dock. He appeared to be washing the sponges. His well-groomed beard glistened in the sunlight. Its red highlights made him even more striking. Bea fought the urge to walk up to him. Again last night he had almost kissed her. Frightened by such raw emotion, she had pulled away from him. Yet, she couldn't stop thinking about what it would be like to kiss—and be kissed—by such a powerful man.

She walked into the small shop featuring handmade crafts from the area residents. There were figurines made from shells, carved coconut husks and a variety of other strange items.

"May I help you?" a medium-height, fortyish woman asked.

"I'm just browsing, thank you." Bea glanced at the shell figurines.

"Take all the time you'd like. My name is Peg; I own this little shop."

"Did you make these?" Bea pointed to the shell critters.

"Actually, those are made by someone else. My hobbies are over there." She motioned to the side wall where various cloth items lined the shelves.

Bea worked her way over. There were linen tablecloths with finely embroidered flowers on the corners, some matching napkins, napkin ring holders, and a variety of rag dolls. "These are wonderful."

"Thank you. I opened the shop during the war. I found the soldiers loved to purchase items to send home to their mothers, wives, and sisters. The island has a certain uniqueness, being so far south. And people seem to like to buy trinkets for loved ones when they travel."

Bea chuckled. "That's why I'm browsing."

"Where are you from, and how long are you here?" Peg sat down behind the counter and brushed back her long blond bangs.

"Came from New York. I'll be returning home as soon as I procure passage."

"New York, as in the city?"

"Oh no, I'm from way upstate, near the Canadian boarder. I brought Richard to his uncle Ellis."

"The nanny. I should have realized. Heard you had a bout with heatstroke."

Did everyone know her business? "Yes. Didn't know if I was going to make it at one point. The doctor said it was because I'm used to the very cold temperatures up North, in contrast to the heat here."

"Happens to a lot of folks—no shame in it. Has Mr. Southard found a new nanny for the child?"

"I don't believe he has, but Richard is a good boy. It shouldn't be difficult."

Peg laughed. "This is Ellis Southard we're talking about, right?"

Bea knitted her eyebrows. "Yes."

"You should have seen his list. The woman had to be a saint and fifty years old at least, according to what he put together. Of course, most of the young gals here were hoping to get the job in order to hook the man. He's just not interested in marriage. And it ain't from a lack of some gals trying, let me tell you."

Bea blushed.

"Sorry, I shouldn't be so forward. Comes from living here so long. People just learn to let their mouths flap a bit. Never did gossip much at home, but here. . .well it's the favorite pastime."

"I understand."

"So, I take it Mr. Southard isn't interested in keeping you on as the child's nanny."

"I have responsibilities back home. My family is planning another coming-out party."

"Coming-out party! You best set yourself down, dear. We've got plenty to discuss." Peg beamed and pointed to a stool.

❧

Ellis worked his shoulders back, easing out the tension. He watched Beatrice make her way around to the various docks and ships. He supposed he could have told her there were none immediately heading to New York, but he wondered if she would have believed him.

She looked wonderful this morning in her Spanish skirt and blouse. The style of clothing fit her and her more aggressive personality. He wondered what some of the high society ladies back home would think if they saw her dressed in such a casual style. "Probably collapse," Ellis chuckled.

She had slipped into Peg Martin's gift shop and seemed to be spending quite a bit of time inside. Peg was a great gal, but she could rattle on so. He wondered if he should go over to the store and rescue Bea from Peg's assault of questions.

" 'Morning, Ellis." Marc Dabny headed toward him.

" 'Morning."

"Heard the lady was leaving the island soon."

"Appears so."

"I asked her if she would like to go to dinner with me one night, but she let me know she would be leaving and was in no position to begin a relationship."

"Sounds wise." She'd given Ellis just the opposite impression. He reminded himself he wasn't interested in pursuing a relationship. She was leaving.

"She's quite a looker," Marc whistled.

"I guess. So tell me, what brings you over this morning, Marc?" He must have spent too much time in the sun; his head was pink from an obvious sunburn, Ellis observed. Why a man with so little hair on his head didn't wear a hat baffled him.

"Oh, right. I was wondering if you had room for a partner."

"Partner?"

"Yeah, I've got some money set aside and I think your business is going to be growing. I also have a couple ideas about expanding your market."

"Haven't given any thought to expanding." In fact, he was beginning to think about closing down the business and returning home to New York to raise Richard on the family farm. "Maybe we should talk, Marc."

Marc rubbed his hands together. "Great. With my investment

we could hire a few more men, buy a few more boats, and begin shipping the sponges into other cities besides New York."

"I'm listening." And Ellis seriously was. If Marc bought into the business, maybe Ellis could return home and still maintain his business here in Key West.

"As you know, the railroad is expanding across the western frontier. And I was thinking, if we took the sponges to the cities where people connect with the trains, we would see the sponges move out west as well."

"Interesting. Do you have contacts in some of these cities?"

"Some. Men I served with in the war. But I could make a trip north, make some contacts and line up initial sales."

Marc was a go-getter, and he seemed to have an eye for business. "Marc, I would need to see your books and how well you manage your assets before I agree."

"And I would like a look at yours as well."

"That's fair. All right, why don't you come over this evening and we'll discuss business in a more formal manner. I'd want a lawyer to draw up any agreement."

"Naturally."

"I must tell you, I might be interested in having someone else run the business so I can return to New York for a while and take care of the farm."

"Either way, you stay and run it or I stay, doesn't much matter. I'll be over after dinner tonight."

"I'll have my books ready," Ellis said and took a step back toward his work.

Marc waved his salutation and left.

Should he move back to New York? Should he raise Richard there? Or should he just stay put and enjoy his life here? So many questions. So many changes in such a short span of time. Ellis sat on the edge of the dock and prayed. "Father, I'm confused. I see advantages to Marc coming on as a partner, but I want to be wise. I want to honor Richard's request to raise his son, and I know he wanted the boy to enjoy growing up on the farm. But can I really return home?

And what about this attraction to Beatrice Smith? If I return to New York won't she be there also?" Ellis groaned.

He sprang up, peeled off his shirt, shoes, and socks, and jumped into the ocean. A long hard swim was in order. He needed some physical exercise. He needed to relax.

❧

"Goodness, you did all that for a friend?" Peg asked.

"Yes, and I'd do it again." Bea sipped a cup of tea Peg had given her.

"That kind of friendship is hard to find. I'm pleased to know you, Bea."

Bea dabbed her mouth with the cloth napkin. "Thanks, I'm sure many folks would do what I did."

"I wouldn't be so sure.

"We have a dinner at the Presbyterian church tonight. Would you like to come?"

"Goodness, what time?"

"Six."

Ellis usually returned home at five. "Sure, I'd love to. Thanks."

"Tell you what, I'll have my brother, Danny, come by your place and escort you to the church."

"If you tell me where it is, I think I can manage it." Bea shifted on the stool.

Peg waved her hand with a quick flick of the wrist. "Nonsense, a woman should have an escort. You know that."

"But I thought such things weren't followed down here."

"True enough, but once the sun goes down and the sailors start to drinking, it's just wise to have a man escort you." Peg tapped her hand onto Bea's.

"I see your point. I'm staying in the cottage in back of Ellis Southard's home."

"The cottage?"

"Don't ask," Bea sighed.

Peg laughed. "Guess it has to do with you not being over fifty, right?"

"Possibly. . .I really don't know. But it is the cutest little cottage. I love it." Bea smiled. "I better get going. Cook will have my hide if I don't return soon. Thanks for the tea and the conversation." Bea slipped off the stool.

" 'Welcome. Next time I'll let you buy something." Peg winked.

Bea giggled and walked out the door. She glanced over at Ellis's dock and saw him jump in the ocean, half naked.

"Oh my!" she exclaimed and turned her head. Her face flushed. She quickened her pace. *Lying in a snow bank might be the best thing at the moment,* she thought. Snow was not to be found in Key West and likely never would be. Bea opened the fan she had brought with her and fanned herself as she walked up Front Street back to Ellis Southard's home.

thirteen

Ellis couldn't believe it. The first evening he was home for dinner in two nights and Beatrice Smith had accepted an invitation to dine at the Presbyterian church. Seeing Peg Martin's brother, Dan, come to escort Bea had him speculating that Peg might have other intentions besides dinner. Pacing back and forth down the hall, stroking his beard, he wondered why the thought bothered him so.

While Richard slept peacefully upstairs, Marc had come and gone, scrutinizing Ellis's books and finding them in order, just as Ellis had found Marc's. It seemed plausible that the two could become partners. Marc's bid to purchase half of the business was a fair market value. But before he moved on with this merger, Ellis wanted and needed references. Truth be told, harvesting and exporting sponges was the furthest thing from his mind.

Listening, waiting for Beatrice's return, drove him into a frenzy of worry. The late hour, along with his inability to go searching for her without waking up the child, left him feeling helpless. The rich mahogany grandfather's clock chimed once, noting it was half past the hour of ten. Perhaps he should wake the boy? He placed his foot on the first step, and then heard laughter. Ellis paused.

Yes, it was definitely laughter, feminine laughter. He eased his foot off the step and sauntered over to the front door. Leaning around the doorjamb he could see the young couple. Beatrice removed her hand from Dan's arm. They were talking; she was smiling, a friendly banter exchanged between them.

Dan bowed slightly and kissed the top of her hand. Fire blazed up Ellis's spine. How dare he be so forward? And yet,

Dan was being the perfect gentleman.

Ellis waited for Dan to leave before he opened the door.

"Hello, Ellis," Bea smiled.

Had she seen him behind the door? "I was wondering if we could talk?"

"I think that would be nice. Shall I come into the big house and we can share a cup of tea?"

"Sure." Ellis slipped back into the house and raised the lights. The warm glow pushed aside some of his earlier dark emotions.

Bea slipped through the open door, the swish of her skirt alerting him to her nearness. He turned. She was beautiful.

"You waited up for me?" she asked and walked past him toward the kitchen.

"Yes. We need to talk."

"Yes, we do." She placed the full teakettle, on the lit stove, then she moved swiftly to the cabinet where the cups were stored, removing two with their saucers. She must have spent more time with Cook than he imagined.

"I had an offer today to buy into my sponge business."

She paused for a moment and asked, "Was it a good offer?" She went back to her work.

"Respectable."

"Do you know and trust the man enough to join into a partnership with him?"

"Marc seems responsible."

"Marc Dabny?" She turned from the counter and faced him.

"Yes."

"And this is the same man that—"

"Yes." Ellis cut her off. He didn't want to be keelhauled all over again for that one.

"And you trust him?" She raised her cinnamon brown eyebrow.

"At this point. Is there something I don't know about him that you would question my judgment so?"

"Seems to me a couple days ago the man was hunting for a wife. Not an ordinary wife, a slave, with a pretty figure, mind you."

"He told you that?"

"Not in so many words, but yes, it was clear to me what the man's intentions were. If a man can treat a woman like that, what kind of a man would he be as a business partner? Would he want you to slave and do all the work while he sat back and enjoyed your profits?"

"I hadn't thought about that." Truth was he hadn't had much room for any thought which didn't revolve around her.

Bea poured the boiling water into the teapot and let it steep. "Why did he want to buy into your business, Ellis?"

"He said he saw room for expansion, and I think he has some valid ideas." There. He wasn't a total idiot when it came to business.

"Well, I don't know the first thing about your business and where it may or may not be expanded. Truth is, I've never heard of a sponge business before. But you seem to be doing well. Would this expansion need the help of another owner?"

"Possibly, possibly not."

Bea set the teapot on a tray with the cups. "Shall we sit in the living room or would you prefer to sit at the table?"

"Living room is fine." Ellis scooped up the tray and led the way.

❧

Bea followed Ellis, noticing how his strong shoulders pressed his white cotton shirt. The man was in excellent shape.

Ellis poured her a cup.

Bea sat on the sofa in front of the cup of tea he had placed on the Queen Anne mahogany table. She smoothed her skirt and waited for Ellis to pour his own tea and sit down. He sat beside her on the sofa. "What do you want to talk about, Ellis?"

"Are you aware of the hour?"

"Yes, and you and I both know you don't want to talk with

me about the time I've returned home."

Ellis tugged at his collar and nodded. He stood up and began to pace. *At least he is working out his thoughts,* she mused.

"Richard said you would be joining us tomorrow morning."

"Yes. After you so wonderfully put it back in my lap."

"What?"

"Richie said that you said to go ask me about fishing with the two of you."

"Oh. Well, I didn't know what to tell the boy, and I certainly wasn't going to be answering for you."

"Thank you."

"Bea, this is crazy. I'm so full of wild emotions I don't know what to think or do. Let alone make sense of anything."

"And you think I understand these emotions?"

He sat down beside her on the sofa. The warmth of him so close to her sent a warm glow radiating within her. *Oh Lord, help me now,* she silently pleaded.

"Ellis, tell me what happened." Without thought, she reached over and touched his sun-darkened hand, tenderly stroking it.

"I'll tell you, but please do not pass judgment on my family for my actions. They were mine and mine alone."

"Very well."

And Ellis began. He told her about Heather, their whirlwind romance, and about the night they stole a passionate kiss. How her hands went beneath his shirt, and how he was driven by desire to go beyond where a gentleman should. And about her father, finding them locked in each other's embrace, and his warning for Ellis to get out of town or he would ruin the reputation of the Southard family name.

"So, you created a stone wall and kept women at bay for all these years?"

"It was the only way. I was so out of control that night."

"I see. And it was all you, right?"

"Of course. I was the one who initiated the kiss."

Bea smiled. "Ellis, in my opinion, unless you force yourself upon us, by and large, women are the ones who send out the signals about wanting or not wanting to be kissed."

"But what about the other night? You and I both know we could have been lost in our passions."

"True, but we weren't. At the right moment, wisdom prevailed and we stopped. Emphasis on the word 'we,' Ellis. You and I both stopped.

"Can I ask you something even more personal?"

Ellis chuckled, "I don't think anything is more personal than what I just admitted to you about myself."

"Were you used to women putting their hands under your shirt?"

His eyebrows arched up into his forehead. "No, it was a completely new experience."

"Did you direct Heather's hands to go there?"

"No." He knitted his eyebrows together.

"Do you see my point yet?" Bea stroked her thumb over Ellis's firm grip.

"I'm not sure. Are you suggesting Heather was the more aggressive person?"

"Yes."

"But I didn't do anything to stop her. She was a sweet, innocent girl before I kissed her."

"Had you kissed many women before Heather?"

"No."

Bea knew Heather O'Donald's reputation, and obviously Ellis didn't. While still a young girl, Bea had heard the whispered news of Heather O'Donald's hurried wedding and soon-delivered first child. And this occurred a year after Ellis left. Obviously, Ellis never knew, or if he did, he probably blamed himself for that as well.

She reached up and stroked his bearded jaw. "Ellis, was it Heather O'Donald, by chance?"

"Yes. But for her sake, please don't repeat any of this."

"I won't. But what I'm going to tell you isn't pretty, and I'll be as gentle as I can. Heather O'Donald married quickly, a year after you left the area, and had a child six months later." Ellis lowered his head and wagged it back and forth.

"It's not your fault."

"Of course it is. Don't you see? If I hadn't kissed her so passionately, she never would have known. . ."

Bea took both of her hands and placed them on his face and lifted it to look at her. "Ellis, I think you were the innocent one. True, you had desires, and perhaps you would have acted upon them. But Heather had desires too. She was bold, far bolder than you. Don't you see?"

"Maybe, but I'm the man. . ."

Bea chuckled. "And only men sin, right?"

He narrowed his gaze.

"Ellis, I always found that when two people sin, both are guilty. God will forgive you, and you can ask Him to forgive Heather. The hardest part is for you to forgive yourself."

"How did you become such a wise woman at such a young age?"

"I'm not. But I do pay attention, and I think what you and I are fighting is an attraction far deeper than your lustful moment with Heather."

❧

Ellis pulled back from Bea's loving embrace. Her words made perfect sense. Had Heather already been exposed to such passions? He thought back on their few dates. She had been the aggressor. She seemed to. . . Ellis cleared his throat. "So, do you think you can trust me with these intense passions?"

Bea turned her head then looked back at him. "Can you trust me?" Her faint blush accented her beauty.

Ellis sat in the chair opposite the sofa. "You're an incredible woman, Beatrice Smith. Not only are you beautiful enough to take my breath away, your mind is quick, and you get to the heart of the matter with a forward resolve I've never seen before."

"Thank you—I think."

Ellis chuckled. "My words were meant as a compliment.

Unlike Marc, I would never want a servant for a wife. I would want a companion, someone who would challenge me, someone with whom I could share my deepest thoughts and concerns. Someone I could trust with my heart."

"Is that a proposal?"

Ellis gulped.

Not giving him a chance to respond, she quipped, "And you say that I'm honest. I've never met a man like you, Ellis. And I must tell you, I like what I see."

Ellis grinned. Was she admitting she found him handsome? "What do we do now?"

"I have no idea." Bea lifted her teacup. It shook in her hand and she immediately nested in back on the saucer.

"You're afraid to be with me, aren't you?"

"Yes. . .no. It's not what you're thinking."

"Explain." Ellis lowered his chin onto his clasped hands with his elbows supported by the arms of the chair.

"Yes, I'm afraid of the attraction between us. No, I'm not afraid of you and your past. You were a boy bursting to be a man. I've heard that it is a difficult time for all young men."

Ellis's cheeks flamed. "It can be."

"I found out today that no ships will be leaving for New York for a while."

"I know."

"You knew?" She knitted her eyebrows.

"I know the comings and goings of ships. It's all a part of my business. I need to find ships to carry my cargo."

"Oh, right. Well, I was going to say, why don't we slowly see what develops between us? You know, spend some time, talking like this."

Ellis smiled. "Yes, I think that would be in order. Shall I come to your cottage tomorrow night after Richard's gone to bed?"

"Why don't we start with some time in public."

"In public? You want me to court you?"

Bea chuckled. "Is that a problem?"

"No, but—"

"But, since the woman is right here in my backyard, why do I need to fuss over her, right?"

She could be forward. He amended his words. "I didn't mean it that way. If you want me to court you, I'll do it." Ellis squirmed, working the tension out of his back.

"No, you don't have to court me. I was merely trying to suggest we spend time together. Like meal time, playing with Richard after dinner, those times. You've been avoiding coming home at dinner since the other night in the cottage."

"Work kept—"

"Ellis!"

"Oh all right, yes. I was thinking up work that needed doing so I didn't have to face you. Better?"

Bea smiled. "Much."

"Oh, you can have a nasty side, I see," Ellis teased.

"Nasty? Me. . .? Now Ellis, whatever gave you that idea?" She winked.

Just what had he gotten himself into? Ellis's fingers tightened around the arms of the chair.

fourteen

Ellis lay in bed as the sun rose. The bright orange glow cast stark shadows over the room. He rubbed his face. "I can't believe I admitted everything to Beatrice last night," he groaned. Granted, she was easy to talk with, but. . . "Marriage? Did I really propose marriage?"

"Lord, I'm certain I didn't. I was just saying if I was to marry. That isn't asking a woman, is it? Do I want to. . .to. . . I can't say it, Lord. The very thought sends shivers of fear up my spine. Although the conversations would be lively with Miss Smith."

Ellis pulled the covers off and sat up, swinging his feet over the edge. He stood and stretched his sore muscles. His bed looked like a battlefield. And a battle of emotions had been waged all night. Did he want to pursue a relationship with Miss Smith, or not? One thing was certain. It would solve the need for a nanny. And Beatrice does love the child. *She isn't an unpleasant woman for a man to get saddled with. . .if a man must be saddled,* he reasoned.

But a wife wasn't a saddle. She was to be cherished, loved, honored, and adored. Could he truly do those things with regard to Beatrice Smith? "I don't know, Lord. I'm so confused. And what's this sixth sense you've given her about Marc? Is there something I don't see?" Ellis paced back and forth in his room.

The gentle knock on his door stopped him mid-stride. "Who is it?"

"Me, Uncle Ellis."

"Come in, Son."

The door creaked open slowly. "Cook says to come to breakfast."

Ellis smiled, confident Cook would pronounce it as an order. "Tell her I'll be right down. I need to shave."

"Shave? You taking off your beard?" Richard questioned, his eyes opened wide, waiting for an answer.

"I may have a beard, Son. But, I do still shave." Ellis pointed to the various places on his face and neck where he did shave. "Plus, I have to keep it trim."

"My daddy didn't wear a beard, just a 'stache."

Ellis grinned. "A 'stache, huh? Do you think I should take off my beard?"

"No, you look like Uncle Ellis with a beard."

Ellis chuckled. Children's logic could be so profound. "You better go tell Cook I'll be right down or she'll have both our hides."

Richard ran out of the room as if lightening would strike. Ellis grinned. The woman did have a way of putting fear into a person. He looked into the mirror. Would Bea prefer no beard? Ellis tried to imagine what his face would look like without it. He'd grown the beard when he was twenty and had never once shaved it off. He remembered her loving touch on his beard last night, cupping his face in her tender hands. Such compassion. Such honesty. No, he'd leave his beard. She certainly didn't seem to have a problem with it.

Ellis finished getting ready for the day and worked his way down the stairs. The lilt of Bea's laughter floated into the hall. He paused, enjoying its merriment, then continued on to the dining room. "Good morning, everyone." He caught a glimpse of Bea, and she flushed slightly. Goodness she was beautiful in the morning. He sat down at the head of the table. Cook was in the kitchen. Richard was buttering his biscuit. Ellis caught Bea's glance and mouthed the words, "You're beautiful."

A deep crimson blush painted her high cheekbones. Ellis smiled and released his gaze. While questions abounded in her absence, in her presence all arguments, fears, and worries dissolved. For the first time in fifteen years he truly felt forgiven for his past, and he owed his inner release to this incredible woman. If only he had learned that lesson before his parents had passed. He would have gone home for a visit. Heather's family's threats were meaningless in the scope of her wedding a year later.

A peace settled within him regarding his parents. They were in heaven. They would know the truth, and one day he would meet them again.

"Uncle Ellis, where are we fishing today?"

"I thought we might go for a sail and fish for some deep-water fish, like kingfish." Ellis picked up the fork with his right hand.

"Fishing on a boat?" Richard bounced up and down with excitement on his chair.

"Yes, we have to sail out quite a distance before we can fish. Would you like that?"

Richard bobbed his head up and down with such vigor, his entire body shook.

"Miss Smith, do you think you can handle the sun for an entire day?" Ellis asked, scooping another forkful of eggs.

"I'm not sure. I've been feeling stronger." Bea's voice seemed uncertain. Was she afraid of being on a boat? No, that couldn't be. . .she had sailed here from New York. Was she afraid of being alone with him for an entire day? But Richard would be with them, he reasoned.

Ellis dabbed his mouth with his napkin, then spread it over his lap again. "There's a small cabin on the boat where you can get some shade."

"I know you didn't ask my advice," Cook interrupted, "but I think a full day's sail might be a bit much for the lady." Cook sat herself down at the table.

"You think so, Cook?" Bea asked, fussing the edge of her napkin with her fingertips.

"I'd be waiting a bit more if it was myself." Cook lowered her head, clasped her hands, and silently prayed over her breakfast.

"I think I'll take Cook's advice and stay here. I'm sorry, Richard, but I won't be fishing with you today."

Ellis straightened in his chair. "We don't need to go deep-sea fishing. We could still use the boat and fish around the island.

"No thank you. You and Richard go ahead. I'll browse some more through town. I barely scratched the surface yesterday."

Richard tattled. "Nanna didn't like the big waves on the boat from New York."

Ellis searched Bea's eyes. "Were you seasick?" he asked.

"A little," Bea admitted.

"Land sakes, child. No wonder the heat got you so bad." Cook tossed her head from side to side and ate some of her eggs.

"Did that matter?" Bea asked.

Ellis couldn't believe his ears. *Did it matter?* he grumbled to himself. "Of course it mattered. You were already a bit dehydrated from the seasickness. No wonder you were hit so hard. I want you to stay home today, and don't be spending too much time in town. We don't want you having a relapse."

"Is that an order or concern?" she rebuffed.

"Ew-wee, I'm not touching that one," Cook giggled, and stood up, removing her plate from the table.

"Concern." Ellis held back his temper.

Richard's head bobbed back and forth between the two of them, then settled on Bea to wait for her response.

"Then I'll not be upset with your concern. And I'll do as you recommend."

Ellis reached over and cupped her hand under his own. "I am concerned, Bea," he whispered.

"Thank you."

❧

Richard knitted his eyebrows together. Bea removed her hand away from Richie's prying eyes. He was trying to figure out what had just happened, and Bea suspected Cook knew exactly what was going on between Ellis and her. "Richie, finish your breakfast so you can go fishing and sailing with your uncle."

"All right." He stabbed his fork into some eggs and gulped them down.

Ellis and she had agreed to take things one step at a time, but he had thrown her with his comment about how beautiful she was. On the other hand, she couldn't help but notice how handsome he was this morning, as well. They would have to decide fast if they were, or were not, going to court. She wasn't sure she could take too much of this.

"All done," Richard proclaimed, and took his empty plate to the kitchen.

"I'm sorry, Ellis," she whispered. "I should have known you were speaking with concern, not orders. I have a tendency to dislike being ordered about."

Ellis grinned. "I'm rather accustomed to women like that. I'll be more careful how I word my thoughts in the future."

"Can I have another offer for a gentle sail around the island?" Bea allowed her hand to travel in Ellis's direction.

He picked up on her cue and cupped her hand again. She breathed in deeply. His warmth and strength blended with his tenderness and found expression in the simple gesture. *Amazing,* she mused.

His voice lowered. "You feel it too?"

She nodded.

"We'll talk some more tonight." Ellis looked back to the kitchen. Cook seemed to have given Richard a chore. "Thank you for last night. I feel so at peace with my past."

"You're welcome."

He squeezed her hand slightly. "Later," he whispered.

Bea nodded and removed her hand. As much as she didn't want to, she knew she had to. Richard was bound to come racing through those doors any minute.

As if on cue, the door banged open. "Uncle Ellis?"

"Yes, Richard." Ellis winked at Bea.

"Cook says I need sailing clothes. What are they?"

"You'll need some oilcloth clothes to you protect from the rain. But we'll be okay today. Just gather a set of warm pants, a shirt, and a sweater or winter coat."

"It's too hot."

"It's in case of a storm on the water, Richard. You need to be prepared."

A storm? Could they run into a storm? Bea implored Ellis's gaze for some assurance.

"Truth be told, there aren't many storms down here in the winter months. Hurricane season is over."

"Hurricanes?"

Ellis chuckled. "An ugly Nor'easter—but these come from the south."

"Oh."

"Go get your change of clothes, Richard. We need to get going if we're going deep-sea fishing."

Richard scurried off.

"Is he safe out there?" Bea asked in Richard's absence.

"He'll be fine."

Bea tried not to worry. She didn't know anything about sailing. Her first sail was on the *Justice.*

"Trust me." Ellis now stood beside her and placed his hand on her shoulder. "We'll be fine."

Bea nodded.

She watched Ellis retreat from the dining room. Bea gathered up the few remaining dishes to take to the kitchen. Cook's remaining in the kitchen meant she was deliberately giving the two of them some privacy. But Cook being Cook, she would have plenty of questions when Bea entered the kitchen. Bea took in a deep breath and pushed the kitchen door open with her hip.

"Here's the rest of the dishes, Cook."

"Thank you. Put 'em by the sink."

"May I help?" Bea offered.

"I'd be a fool to turn down a good offer. Water's hot, you can start washing."

And Bea went straight to work.

"Nanna," Richard yelled.

"In the kitchen," she called back.

" 'Bye. Uncle Ellis said we'd be gone until supper."

Bea wrapped her damp arms around Richard and gave him a great big bear hug and groaned, "Have fun, Richie."

Richard ran out of the kitchen and grasped his uncle's hand.

"He sure took to his uncle," Cook said.

"There seems to be a connection." Bea went back to the dishes.

"Seems to be one between Mr. Ellis and you, too."

Ugh, here it comes. Bea continued to scrub. What could she say?

"I told the man to make peace with you, I didn't tell him to. . ."

Bea rewashed the plate for the second time. "Oh, for pity sakes, Cook. We're just. . ."

"Just?"

"Oh, all right, we're attracted to each other."

"If you don't mind me saying so, I knew it." Cook's grin slipped up to her eyes, causing them to sparkle.

"What?"

Cook laughed. "I could tell the first time I saw you. You were smitten by Mr. Ellis. Thing is, I've seen that in other young ladies before. But I must say, you're the first one to ever have him return the interest."

"We're going to take it slow. Be friends. See if anything develops."

Cook continued to laugh as she cleaned her counter. "I say you'll be married before the end of the month."

The woman was crazy. The end of the month was next week. There was no way she and Ellis would. . .well, maybe it was possible. A flicker of desire stirred in Beatrice. She thanked the Lord she wasn't facing Cook and closed her eyes to calm her emotions.

"Do you love him?" Cook tenderly asked. Having come up beside her, she placed her firm hands on Bea's shoulders.

Bea turned and faced her. "I don't know. I can't say what it is I'm feeling for him."

"Give it time, child. Give it time."

"I don't know what to do, Cook. I'm supposed to go home in a few days. I can't very well stay here in his house or even his cottage if we're courting. It wouldn't be right. And yet, I don't have a job to support myself and stay on the island. I have some funds saved, but they're back home in a bank."

"Like I said, give it time. The Good Lord understands all your needs, desires, and confusion. He'll help you out."

Bea sighed. "I was up most of the night praying. I've never been so attracted to a man, and yet is that grounds to get married?"

Cook's eyebrows went up. "He asked you?"

"Well no, not exactly, but the subject did come up."

"Land sakes, he's hit worse than I thought." Cook slipped her arm around Bea's back and led her to a chair at the kitchen table. "Mr. Ellis has been asking me to move in ever since he bought this place. Guess maybe the time's come."

"What about your family?" Bea asked.

"They could use my room for some of those younguns who's growing up. I'll start moving my things in today."

"Don't you think we ought to approach Ellis about this?"

"Fiddlesticks. I won't let silly town gossip compromise him or you. I'll move in, and you stay in the cottage."

Bea giggled. "That's an order, isn't it?"

"Yup, and I'll be watching you two. Don't you worry yourself none. With me and the Good Lord, you'll be behaving yourselves."

Bea laughed and threw her arms around Cook. "Thank you. You don't know how much your being here will help."

"I believe I do, child. I was young once, too."

Bea flushed.

Cook roared with laughter. "I say, you young folks have a terrible time realizing us older ones were ever your age."

"With you around, Cook, I don't think I'll be forgetting it."

"Good. Well, if I'm moving in today, you'll be giving me a hand."

Bea gave a mock salute. "Aye, aye, Captain."

fifteen

"I like the waves, Uncle Ellis," Richard hollered, standing on the bench of the sailboat.

"Richard, get down, now!" Ellis roared. The surf rocked the boat and battered the hull as it crashed down on the waves.

Richard slipped back down on the bench. "But it's fun standing up," he pouted.

"It may be fun, Son, but it is dangerous. If you're going to sail with me, you have to obey the rules."

"Yes, sir. I'm sorry." Richard lowered his head and looked at his dangling feet.

"Thank you. Now, it's time to go back home. The sun is low on the horizon.

"But I didn't catch a big one, like you."

"Next time." If there was a next time. He had no idea how hard it would be to keep a four year old contained on a boat. And it wasn't that big of a boat. Yet, he still managed to get into everything. Ellis's nerves were shot. Not with the child, but with the fear that somcthing might happen to him. He would only take him again if he brought Bea along. She could help watch Richard.

Ellis turned the bow toward Key West and began the long sail back to the island.

"Richard, cast your rod, let's see if you catch anything on the way home."

His head bobbed up and down as he picked up his rod and placed it over the side, letting the line go out further and further.

"That's enough, Son."

Richard secured his rod and placed it in the mounts Ellis had, put into the boat long ago. Richard laid back on the bench and watched the top of the rod to see if he snagged a fish.

"Uncle Ellis?"

"What, Son?"

"Do you like Nanna?"

Oh dear, the child had caught him placing his hand upon Bea's. "Yes, she's a nice lady." There. *That's honest, and not too leading,* he thought. He hoped.

Placing his hands behind his head, Richard leaned back and said, "Are you going to marry Nanna?"

Ellis held back an audible groan. "I don't know. Why do you ask, Son?"

"Billy's mommy and daddy hold hands, and they're married."

"Holding hands doesn't mean a man and woman are married."

"Oh." Richard sat up. "What makes a man and woman married?"

"First, they have to love each other."

"Do you love Nanna?"

Ellis closed his eyes and whispered a silent prayer for guidance. "I don't know. Nanna and I just met. We need to get to know one another. Love has to develop, it doesn't just happen overnight." While he had felt an instant attraction to Bea the first time he met her, he wouldn't call such an attraction love. On the other hand, his feelings for her today were far stronger and closer to love than attraction.

"So if a man and woman love each other, they're married?"

"No, they have to decide they want to get married."

Richard knitted his eyebrows.

Ellis continued. "A man and a woman have to go to a preacher to 'get' married. When they do that the preacher declares them married, and they kiss."

"Have you kissed Nanna?"

The sudden intense heat on Ellis's cheeks made him acutely aware he was blushing. "No, Son. I haven't."

"I love you, Uncle Ellis. And I love Nanna. If you get married, we'll be a family, like Billy's."

Ellis couldn't respond. The child longed for a family like his friend back home. A part of Ellis would love to jump in and marry Bea just to give the child some security. But marriage was far too serious of a venture to jump in for the wrong reasons. What would happen after Richard was grown? Would they separate, no longer needing to be together, or would they slowly grow in love with each other? No, Ellis resolved. The child needed stability, and he wasn't going to jump into a marriage unless love, friendship, and honesty were a part of it right from the very start.

"Richie, look—a porpoise jumping in the waves." Ellis pointed to the gray bottle-nosed dolphin near the bow of the boat. "They're swimming with us."

"Wow." Richie leaned over the side. Ellis grabbed the boy by his britches and held him fast. *Thank You, Lord, for dolphins.*

❧

Bea couldn't believe the pack of children gathered at Cook's home. It was a simple home, clean and well-kept. Several bedrooms ran along the left side of the house, while a large living area, dining area, and small kitchen ran along the right side. Little brown children of all shapes and sizes looked at Bea. *No wonder Cook runs things with a firm hand,* she reasoned.

"Grandma, can I have your room?" a young girl with braided hair pleaded.

"It'll be up to your parents. But you can't move in until I move my things to Mr. Ellis's house."

The young girl nodded and walked off.

"That's Darlene. She's the oldest of my son George's children. That's Ben, he's eight, and my daughter Lizzy's oldest." Cook pointed to a thin boy with a wide grin.

"How many live here?" Bea questioned.

"Let me see. . .George, his wife and their three children, Lizzy and her four children. Lizzy's husband died fighting in the war. And myself, so I guess that makes eleven."

More than seven children filled the house. Bea slowly scanned and counted the children. Cook laughed. "Kids from around the island come here for Lizzy to teach 'em some math and reading."

"Oh."

"We try to pass on to the children things they'll need in the future." Cook walked down the hall to the back bedroom.

"I might have some books Lizzy could use," Bea volunteered. "I bought them for Richard."

"That'd be nice, dear. Let's get to packing my clothes. We've got a heap of work to do."

"Grandma, can I help?" Ben asked.

"Sure can. I'll be needing your strong arms to help me carry some of my things to Mr. Southard's house."

"Mother, are you certain?" the tall, thin, elegant woman asked.

"Quite. Lizzy. You know I'll still be over here pestering you. Don't you worry none."

Lizzy laughed. "I'm sure."

"Forgive me my manners. Bea, this is my daughter, Lizzy. Lizzy, this is Bea Smith."

"Hello." Bea reached out to shake Lizzy's hand.

Hesitantly Lizzy reached hers out. When Bea gave her a firm handshake, Lizzy smiled. "A white woman who's not afraid. I like you."

Bea laughed. "Your mom's a gem, but I'm sure you know that."

"She certainly can be. Other times she can be a real nag. Don't try and keep a secret from her."

Bea continued in her laughter. "I've already discovered that."

The three women wrapped some of Cook's clothes into a quilt. With the three of them it didn't take long to pack everything. Soon Bea found herself and Cook unpacking everything in Cook's new room.

"Sure takes longer to unpack," Bea commented, placing a dress on a hanger in Cook's closet.

"Mr. Ellis will sure be surprised," Cook giggled. "He'll think I got a touch of the heat."

Bea laughed. Having Cook around would be a blessing in more ways than one. "I like your family."

"Lizzy seemed impressed with you. You being from the North you might not be aware, but a lot of white folks don't touch colored folks."

"Oh, I'm aware. I'm afraid that's a problem in the North as well. Even with the war being fought."

"Sin is a pretty hard thing to rid from a man's heart," Cook wisely proposed.

"You know, I hadn't thought it was sin, just man being foolish and proud in ways he ought not. But you're right, it is sin. The Bible does say we're all from Adam and Eve, so we all have the same parents." Bea folded the quilt and placed it at the foot of the four-poster bed.

"I believe it's goin' ta take people some time to change, but one day I think most folks will realize that, like President Lincoln said at the Gettysburg Address, 'all men are created equal.' "

"It was a sad day when he was shot," Bea whispered. It had been seven months since the president's assassination.

"That be true, a lot of people still mourn his death." Cook paused and took a deep breath.

Three chimes rang out from the grandfather clock down the hall. "Goodness, child. I better be fixin' dinner."

"You don't think they'll catch anything?"

"Oh, I reckon they'll catch some. But Mr. Ellis likes more than fish for his supper. I may just fix him some black beans and rice. I canned up some beans this summer."

"I don't believe I've ever had black beans."

"Ewww, child, are you in for a treat. Could you fetch me a few tangerines for a sauce for the fish? If'n I know Mr. Ellis, he's caught some kingfish, and he loves this tangerine sauce I make as a marinade for the fish."

"Sounds wonderful. How many?" Bea headed for the door.

"Fetch me a half a dozen," Cook said, brushing the dust off her hands.

❧

The evening breeze brought the sailboat gently into the harbor. Richard was asleep. The porpoises had followed the boat, playing for at least an hour before turning back to the sea. Ellis loved hearing Richard's laughter. And he enjoyed the contentment on the child's face as he slept. The sailboat slowly slid into place alongside the dock. Ellis captured a piling and held the boat fast while he draped a line around it.

In short order he lowered the sails, wrapped the mainsail around the boom, and put the jib into a sack, tossing it through the hold into the bow.

Should I wake the child or let him sleep? he wondered.

"Richard." He sat down on the bench beside the small boy. "Wake up, Son."

Richard groaned and rolled to his side.

Ellis smiled. The ocean had a way of relaxing a person. Often he would end up taking a nap after a good sail. He hoisted Richard up and held him firmly, the boy's head resting on his shoulder. Ellis kissed him tenderly on his soft curls. It was hard to believe how much love he had for this child in only a few short days.

With his free hand, he lifted the fish for the evening's dinner. Taking a giant step from the boat's deck to the dock, he steadied his feet on land once again.

Ellis soon found himself a bit winded as he carried the child the entire distance to the house.

Bea greeted him at the door. A warmth spiraled down his back to the tip of his toes. She was a welcome sight to return home too. "Hi," he smiled.

"Hi. Is Richie all right?" Bea tenderly touched Richard's back.

"Fine, just exhausted and relaxed." Ellis handed her the

fish. "Take these, and I'll put him to bed."

"All right. Don't forget to remove his shoes."

"Yes, ma'am." Ellis winked.

"Sorry—habit." Bea grabbed the fish.

"By the way, I look forward to our time alone tonight," Ellis whispered.

A soft pink rose on Bea's cheeks. "We have a lot to talk about. Come to the kitchen after you put Richard down on his bed and wash up."

Something in the tone of her voice made him question what else had transpired today. He wasn't certain what it meant. "All right," Ellis said with apprehension.

Slowly he worked his way up the stairs, skipping his normal pattern of taking two steps at a time. He didn't want to jostle Richard and possibly wake him up.

Ellis tenderly placed Richard on his bed, pulled off his shoes, and unbuttoned the top button of his shirt. Richard stirred slightly and rolled himself into a curled position. Silently Ellis departed.

In his room he made quick work of changing his shirt and washing the fishy smell from his hands. He sniffed his clean hands, but a pungent odor still remained. His nose crinkled. A desire to smell fresh and clean for Bea encouraged a second washing.

Downstairs he found Bea and Cook working side by side. " 'Evening, ladies."

" 'Evenin', Mr. Ellis." Cook continued to fillet the fish. "I've done what you asked me to do."

"And what is that, Cook?" Ellis leaned against the counter.

"I've moved in."

"What? I mean, that's wonderful. But what brought the sudden change?" Ellis looked at Bea. Bea's face crimsoned.

❧

Ellis shifted his gaze back to Cook.

"Miss Smith and I were talkin'—"

"And?" Ellis cut her off.

"I'll be gettin' to it, now hold on." Cook smiled. "As I said, we were talkin', and we decided it would be best for you to have me in the house."

"I see." Ellis looked at Bea.

"Ellis, you aren't truly upset about this, are you?" Bea implored.

"No, I've been asking Cook to move in with me ever since I bought the house. Far too much room here for one man, and her home could use another open bed." Ellis smoothed his beard. "I'm just surprised."

But why was he surprised, really? Cook could get anything out of anyone. And he had openly touched Bea's hand this morning.

"Do you need me to haul over your belongings, Cook?"

"No sir, we moved 'most everything this afternoon. I don't see no need to take my linens, fine china, and stuff. The family will need it, and you have plenty here."

"True. But I would've moved your belongings." Ellis pushed himself away from the counter and sauntered over to the table where he saw the kingfish fillets marinating in Cook's tangerine sauce. "My favorite, thanks."

"You're welcome." Cook smiled.

Bea remained quiet and continued to work. Besides the need to report on his conversation with Richard, they needed to discuss her conversation with Cook.

Ellis rubbed his hands together and asked, "What can I do to help?"

❧

Bea sat pensively still throughout dinner. She wasn't certain how to read Ellis. He seemed glad that Cook had moved in, but it appeared as if he had something on his mind. He left obvious holes in his description of the fishing excursion with Richard.

Richard woke as everyone was finishing up their meal. Bea sat with Richie as Cook and Ellis went off for an inspection of Cook's new room.

"Nanna, you should have seen 'em. They jump in the waves and swim really fast," Richie excitedly explained about the porpoises. "Uncle Ellis says they breathe air like we do. They have a hole on top of their heads and everything."

"Wow, you had quite a trip." Bea smiled.

"I didn't catch any fish, but Uncle Ellis said sometimes deep-sea fishing is like that." Richard scooped another forkful of his fish dinner. "Isn't this good, Nanna?"

"Yes. Now don't talk with your mouth full, please."

"Sorry," he mumbled through a mouthful of fish.

Bea stifled a chuckle, especially when Richard took up the linen napkin and wiped his mouth, trying to be so grown up.

"Nanna, do you like Uncle Ellis?"

Oh dear, nothing like the direct approach. "Yes."

"Are you going to marry him?"

Bea shifted nervously in her seat. *This isn't conversation for a four year old,* she thought. "I don't know if I like him that way yet."

"What way?"

Bea eased out a pensive breath. "Richie, there are many kinds of love. For example, I love you and I love my parents, but it's not the same kind of love a man and woman need to share to get married."

"When will you know?"

Bea smiled. "I don't know. I suppose when the Lord tells me so."

"Is that when you'll go to church and get married?"

Church? Getting married? What was going on in this little one's mind? "Where are all these questions coming from, Richie?"

"I saw you hold hands with Uncle Ellis, and Billy's parents hold hands."

"I see. Do I hold hands with you?"

Richie nodded.

"Are we going to get married?"

Richie's eyebrows knitted.

"Do you see, Richie? Not everyone who holds hands is getting married."

"Oh. But Uncle Ellis said he likes you."

So, he had spoken with Ellis about this too. "Richie, am I good about doing what's best for you?"

"Uh-huh."

"Then trust me to take care of marriage and other grown-up kinds of things."

"All right." Richie went back to eating his supper. The child was far too observant.

A warm feeling of being watched flowed over the back of her neck. She turned and saw Ellis's handsome figure casually leaning against the doorjamb. A mischievous smile and a wink sent her heart racing in anticipation of their evening's conversation. A lot had transpired since last night, and her desire to get to know him had increased a hundredfold. Was it possible to fall in love at the mere sight of a man?

Bea broke her gaze and fixed it back on Richie who was finishing his rice and beans. "After you're done, Richie, do you want to play a game, perhaps checkers?"

"I beat Uncle Ellis."

"Oh really? Perhaps I'll challenge him to a game later." Bea turned to Ellis, softly lowered her eyelids, and slowly opened them. Flirting. At her age. She could hardly believe it, and yet it felt so right.

Ellis cleared his throat and slipped into the darkened hallway.

sixteen

"Is he asleep?" Bea asked as Ellis descended the stairs.

"Soon. He's exhausted. Three checker games plus all those questions would wear anyone out. Have you encouraged him to ask so many questions?" Ellis sat on the chair opposite the sofa.

"He seemed to come by his curiosity naturally. I was going to ask if you or your brother were inquisitive children."

"Not that I'm aware, but I've been gaining a new prospective since Richard moved in here. I used to think I was a well-behaved child, but as I've questioned some of Richard's behavior, I remember being scolded in some of the same ways." Ellis reclined in the chair, stretched his legs, and crossing them at the ankles.

"Richie seemed to have had the 'love and marriage' question discussion with you earlier," Bea started.

"I think sitting on a hundred tacks would have been easier than dealing with his questions. By the way, you handled it better than I."

Bea laughed. "I've had a bit more experience. I found you don't have to give all the details to the innocent questions he's asking."

"I've got so much to learn." Ellis wrung his hands. "I thought I handled it well, but we ended up talking about church weddings, and other unnecessary details."

"Speaking of church, are we going in the morning?" Bea intended to go to the Presbyterian church with her newfound friends, if Ellis wasn't planning to attend a morning service.

"I was planning on going. Would you like to accompany us?"

"As in a date?" Bea teased.

"You realize things are happening fast between us," Ellis said.

"Things will slow down now that we have admitted to each other what we're feeling." Bea hoped her words were true. She certainly hadn't told him all of her thoughts, and suspected he hadn't told her all of his.

"Maybe." Ellis sat up straight in the chair. "Is Cook intending to be our chaperone?"

"In a manner of speaking, yes. Ellis, I couldn't have stayed in the cottage if we do start courting. It wouldn't be right. And gossip spreads faster on this island than a hailstorm covers the cornfields back home."

Ellis laughed. "That's true enough. I'm glad she moved in. I planned to have her stop coming for breakfast if she didn't. I didn't want her walking the streets before dawn. The island is pretty safe, but we get all kinds of ships in port from time to time, so you never know what sort of sailors will come ashore."

"You've a good heart, Ellis."

"Thank you. Yours isn't so bad either. I've never known Cook to let anyone into her kitchen, and yet, you seem so at home there."

Bea enjoyed working in the kitchen, and Cook was fun to work with. "I like her. She's unique."

Ellis roared. "That she is. So, how long did it take for Cook to get the details from last night out of you?"

Bea felt the heat rise on her cheeks. "Maybe five minutes."

❧

"She's slipping."

"I heard that, Mr. Ellis," Cook called from down the hall.

"Then come and join us so you can hear it all without straining." Ellis stood to await Cook's entrance into the room. He leaned over to Bea and whispered, "I want her to feel comfortable in my home."

Bea nodded.

Ellis pulled away quickly. The smell of lilac in her hair, so soft, so feminine, stirred a desire to kiss her behind her right ear. Thankfully, he constrained himself before he acted on his impulses.

"Are you certain, Mr. Ellis?" Cook slowly entered the room.

"Cook. . .Francine. . .this is your home now. You're always welcome."

Ellis watched Cook's imploring gaze. "Come, sit beside Bea. You've worked hard today." He held her by the hand and led her to the sofa.

"Good thing Master Richard be in bed, he'd have us getting married," Cook giggled.

The room erupted into laughter. The rest of the evening was spent enjoying each other's company—getting to know one another. At ten, Bea stood.

"I don't know when I've enjoyed myself more. It's been a wonderful night, but I must get some rest." Bea bid the others a good night.

"Land sakes, I don't believe the hour. I would have been in bed for an hour if I was home." Cook lifted her ample body off the sofa.

Ellis rose. "May I escort you to your door, Bea?"

"That would be nice, thank you."

"I'll see you young folks in the morning. Behave yourselves." Cook winked and headed down the hall to her room.

Ellis wrapped his arm around Bea's narrow waist. It felt right. Bea leaned into his shoulder and sighed.

I could grow accustomed to this, Ellis thought. *Quite accustomed.*

"Take me home, Ellis, before I fall asleep standing up," Bea whispered.

Ellis squeezed her tightly and led her through the front door, down the steps and to her front door. "I would like to court you, Bea. May I?"

"Will courting be enough? It seems so shallow to what we are already experiencing."

"Perhaps, but you deserve to be treated like a lady. I'll

speak with Cook to arrange an evening when I can take you out on the town and she can watch Richard." Ellis didn't release his grasp of her waist. She turned in his arm to face him.

"I'd like to go out with you." Bea's smile affected him so that his own smile swelled. "You're an incredible woman, Beatrice Smith. I think I'm falling in love with you."

"Oh, Ellis." Bea buried her head in his chest.

Ellis wrapped her tenderly in his arms.

"How can this be happening so quickly?" Bea mumbled into his thick cotton shirt.

"I don't have a clue, darling. But I'm not inclined to fight it any longer, are you?"

"No. I'm scared."

"Me too."

Ellis held her as she trembled in his arms. How is it that love, if this was love, could be so frightening? Was it merely the fact he was ready to throw all his plans aside to pursue a relationship with a person he barely knew? Yes, that's what terrified him so. The thought of being with Beatrice the rest of his life wasn't scary, that was comforting. Yet the ramifications of it were a bit daunting.

❧

Bea placed her hands on his chest and pushed herself back from his grasp. "I should go to bed."

"Good night, Bea." Ellis lifted her right hand and placed a gentle kiss upon it.

"Sleep well, Ellis." Bea gently removed her hand from his embrace and reached for the latch. But Ellis was faster. His hands already set on the latch, he opened the door for her. Reluctantly, she placed one foot in front of the other and entered her darkened cabin.

The door closed behind her. She listened as Ellis's footsteps disappeared into the distance.

"Father, I think I love him. How is it possible?" she called out to God. Not bothering to light her lanterns, she made her way in the dark to her room. "And how can I feel so differently about him than when I first met him a little over a week ago? I don't know how, Lord, but I do. And I know I'm wanting to be with him night and day, wrapped in his arms. Is love like this possible?"

Bea readied herself for sleep. She lit the lamp beside her bed and opened her Bible. In spite of the late hour she needed to go to bed with the Word of the Lord on her mind. She absentmindedly opened the Bible, and it opened to Ecclesiastes 3:5, "A time to embrace and a time to refrain from embracing." Had her time for embracing come? Was Ellis the man God had chosen for her life partner?

❧

The Lord's Day had come, and church with Ellis and Richard gave Bea a hope that maybe they would become a family. The afternoon was spent reading and playing with Richard. Cook spent the day with her family, so Bea prepared the evening meal. It was the first full meal she had made since her departure from the Southard farmstead. A roasted chicken with cornbread stuffing, mashed potatoes, and carrots rounded out the fare.

Cook returned soon after they finished their dinner. "Smells good in here, child."

"Thank you. How was your visit home?"

"Just fine. The older girls were given my room. They had to show me. They were so excited." Cook grinned.

"Do you miss them?" Bea asked, with her arms up to the elbows in dishwater.

"Sure enough do, but this is best. Now they can come and visit me. I told 'em all about sitting in Mr. Ellis's fancy parlor last night, and they can't wait to come see it."

"I'm sure Ellis won't mind." Bea reached for another plate and placed it in the hot soapy water.

"He's the one who told me to invite 'em. Fact is, he wants them here for dinner on Tuesday."

"Tuesday? The whole family?" Bea wondered where they would put everyone.

Cook chuckled. "The whole family. He said he was going to do a barbecue, and you know what that means."

"He's cooking?"

"Yes'm, for the whole lot of 'em. I thought Lizzy was going to fall off her chair when I made the announcement."

Bea laughed.

"I'm used to Mr. Ellis cooking for me a time or two, but my family, well let's just say it'll be a new experience."

"I can imagine." Bea wondered what was going on in Lizzy's mind.

"How was church?" Cook asked, putting on her apron.

"It was fine. Cook, I can handle the dishes. You relax."

"I'm sure you can, but my family waited on me hand and foot like I was the Queen Mother. I need to do something useful today or I think I'll burst."

Bea removed her hands from the water and stepped back from the sink. "I never liked doing dishes." Bea dried off her hands.

Cook chuckled and plunged her hands into the soapy water. "I think we're going to get along real fine, Miss Smith, real fine."

And Bea could picture herself as the woman of this household working alongside Cook. It was a pleasant picture. Her heart warmed, her lips turning up in a smile.

❧

Ellis caught a glimpse of Bea working in the kitchen with Cook. She fit right in, and she looked mighty pretty today. Her hair was up in a bun, but she allowed a few wisps of hair to come down in ringlets alongside her cheeks. One day he was going to run his fingers through that wonderful crown she wore.

"Uncle Ellis?" Richard tugged on his pant leg.

Ellis turned to see the imploring gaze of his nephew, who jumped up and down, wiggling like he had to go to the bathroom.

"Is there a problem, Richard?"

"There's a monster in the outhouse."

"A monster?"

Richard nodded and continued the wiggling.

"Let's go check it out." Ellis grabbed a lantern. He'd found large geckos in the outhouse before. To a four year old, a two- to three-foot gecko could be pretty scary. On the other hand, he was proud that Richard hadn't yelled upon first spotting the creature.

Richard's grasp of Ellis's hand tightened the closer they came to the outhouse. "Stand behind me, Son." Ellis waited until Richard was behind him before he pulled the door open. The bright flash of light caused the gecko to scurry away.

"What was that?" Richard cried.

"A gecko, an overgrown lizard." Ellis encouraged the child to make use of the outhouse. "I'll wait for you."

Richard nodded and stepped inside. Moments later the door swung open and Richard reappeared.

"Uncle Ellis?"

"Yes, Son?"

"Do guckos hurt people?"

"Geckos," he corrected. And no, they don't. Some folks keep them as pets, others eat 'em?"

Richard's eyes grew wide. "They eat 'em?"

"Uh-huh." Ellis grinned. "Some say it tastes like chicken."

"Chicken? That's silly. It didn't have feathers."

Ellis grabbed the boy and tossed him into the air. "That's right, Son, they don't have feathers."

Ellis removed the lantern he had hung on the hook to the left of the door. He couldn't imagine what Bea would have done if she had seen the gecko. Most women would scream, but he'd seen enough of Beatrice to doubt what her immediate response would have been.

"Come on, Son. Let's go play a game of checkers before you go to bed."

"I'll beat you." Richard beamed.

Maybe it was time for Ellis to win a game. He placed Richard on his shoulders and ran to the front of the house, bouncing and jumping. Richard squealed with laughter. Ellis loved children, and he wondered what it would be like to have some of his own. An image of Bea swollen with child burned a desire within him. *Could it be possible, Lord?*

❧

Ellis watched as Bea descended the stairs, having put Richard to bed for the evening. Pleasure radiated from her. "Thank you, Ellis. It meant a lot to me to be able to put him down for the night."

"I know. I cherish my time with him also." He patted the sofa for her to sit down beside him. "Cook's retired early tonight."

"Then maybe I should sit on the chair," Bea suggested, and paused in the center of the room.

"I promise to be the perfect gentleman," Ellis implored. He wanted her close tonight. So much had developed between them in such a short span of time. "Please."

"Ellis." Bea sat down beside him. "Don't you understand? I want this too much."

"Trust me, Bea. I'll be strong for the both of us."

She sat back and he placed his left arm around her shoulders, encouraging her to rest her head on his shoulder. He breathed in the sweet gentle scent of lilac.

"I enjoyed the message from Pastor Williams today. Can you believe he has all those children?"

Ellis chuckled. "Eight is a handful. Do you want children?"

"Yes. I don't think I'd want eight, though." Bea folded her hands in her lap.

"I'm not sure I want eight either, but I'd like a few. How many do you want?" Ellis raised his hand and captured a ringlet of hair, which rested on her cheek. Chocolate silk best described the sensation.

"Truthfully, I'll take as many as the Lord gives. But I think four is a good number."

"Hmm, four, huh?" Ellis whispered.

❧

Bea lifted her head from his shoulder and looked into his blue-gray eyes. They were dark, yet as open and revealing as his soul. "Ellis, what's behind these questions?"

"If you and I should decide to. . .uh, hmm. . .tie the knot, I thought maybe we ought to find out how we feel about children, raising them, our goals, desires, plans, and all that sort of stuff. Like what Pastor Williams spoke about this morning, being prepared in season and out of season."

Bea sat up straight and grasped his hand. "I love children, as you can tell. I believe in being firm with discipline, but I also believe a child should have time to play, enjoy life.

"And you?"

"The same. What about planning for their futures?" Ellis moved his thumbs gently over her fingers.

"I think children should decide their careers. My parents encouraged me in some of my talents even though they're traditionally more male."

"Such as?"

"I have a mind for numbers, business. Father allowed me to learn some of his business and keeping records and such. He said any man would be proud to have a wife who could keep a budget. Truthfully, the skill was handy with your brother being off to war."

"I can well imagine." Ellis shifted and faced her. "Why is it that the more I get to know you, the more I like who you are, Beatrice?"

"Probably because it is the same with me. I thought you were an uncaring, rigid man the first day I met you." Bea paused. Seeing he wasn't offended, she continued. "I soon learned that it was me who you were rigid around. Little did I know you were fighting the same attraction I was."

"And we fought it so well," Ellis chuckled.

Bea struggled for neutral territory. "So we're agreed on children, what about foods?"

seventeen

Monday came and went with an odd sensation of normalcy. Tuesday, Bea found herself immersed in the preparations for the barbecue for Cook's family. "Where are we going to get all the tables and chairs?" Bea inquired of Cook. "I can't believe he invited his crew and their families too."

"I think Mr. Ellis has done freed his heart," Cook laughed.

"Well, I think he's lost his head," Bea proclaimed.

"Same thing." Cook waddled over to the stove. As she lifted the lid, steam billowed into the air.

"What did you call that again? Yucka?"

Cook wagged her head, "No dear. Yucca. It's a root like your potatoes, but we serve it the Cuban way with a garlic sauce poured on top." A fresh aroma of garlic permeated the room as Cook opened the lid of a small pot on the stove.

The food, the trees, everything is so different here—even the fruit, Bea reflected. She loved the passion fruit Cook had been serving for breakfast, but had been avoiding it for fear there was something to its name. "I thought Ellis was going to be doing all the cooking?" Bea pushed back a stray wisp of her hair.

"He's paying and he's doing the barbecue. The men don't think in terms of the whole meal. Unless of course it's missing on his plate."

Bea laughed. "I'm just grateful that the other families are bringing some side dishes as well. We should've started cooking a week ago for such a big crowd." Bea shaped the bread dough into rolls and placed them on the baking pan. She wiped the sweat from her brow. "I can see why the original owners put a kitchen outside—it gets down right exhausting in here."

Cook's worried gaze searched her own eyes.

"I'm fine," Bea responded.

"Nonsense child. Drink some water."

Obediently, Bea downed a glass of water and poured herself another to slowly sip.

"We'll have some time after the food is ready to freshen up. I want you to strip right down and cool yourself off, you hear me?" Cook wagged her finger.

"Yes, ma'am."

"Don't need you getting all faint, no siree," Cook mumbled.

"I'm fine, Cook, really." A simple nod of Cook's head for a response was all that Bea received. She was fine. She caught a glimpse of herself in the glass, her color normal. Sweating was natural from the heat, she reminded herself. Cook was just being overly cautious.

Bea finished shaping the rolls and placed a clean cloth over them to let them rise. Wiping her hands on her apron, she began rolling piecrusts, placing them in the tins. "Where'd you get all these pie tins?" Bea asked.

"Oh, I asked around. A few from my home, and Mrs. Matlin, you remember her?"

"Yes." How could she forget the woman and the tender mercy she'd shown to her last week when she had pushed herself too soon after being sick?

"Oh, by the way, she'll be joining us too."

Bea threw up her hands. "Is there anyone on the island not coming?"

"Not used to crowds, are you dear?"

"No."

"Well here on the island things kinda have a way of growing like this." Cook lifted the large pot of boiling yucca from the stove and brought it to the sink.

"I see." Bea encouraged the pie dough into a circle.

"You'll get used to it. Island folk, we all know each other, and depend on each other. It's a matter of survival. Nowadays, it doesn't seem as much so. But wait 'til we have a storm. Then you'll see how we all pull together."

Like a real community, Bea mused. Being so far out with Richard's homestead, she hadn't been a part of a community for a long time.

"Don't be surprised if'n you see some folks here that we didn't invite. They'll be bringing some of their own food."

Bea closed her eyes and rubbed her palms on her shirt. To go to someone's house uninvited broke all the rules of social graces. Bea couldn't imagine such an impropriety. "What's Ellis doing out there?"

"Roasting the pig. He started it last night."

❧

Ellis turned the pig on the spit once more. He still had enough time to run to town and order the fresh fish. One of his men was bringing conch chowder. At last count, he figured there would be close to thirty coming to dinner. But he'd been to enough occasions on the island to know that number could double in an hour.

He locked the spit in place and hurried to town. Across the street was a teenaged boy he knew. "Hey, Brian, do you have a minute?"

"Sure, what do you need, Mr. Southard?"

The lean boy with a crop of long, black hair walked across the street.

"Can you run an errand for me?"

"Sure."

"Could you fetch a twenty-five pound bag of rice and a mess of fresh vegetables from the store and bring them to my house?"

"It'd be my pleasure." The lad smiled. "Party?"

Ellis chuckled. "Yup. Wanna come?"

"Sure."

"Tell you what, if you can get your mom to cook a couple pies and a mess of that rice for me, your whole family is invited. I'm roasting a pig, picking up a mess of fresh fish and possibly some steaks if the butcher has some."

"I'll let Mom know."

Ellis handed Brian some money and proceeded to the docks. He spoke with a couple of the local fishermen. After he had purchased some fresh fish, he noticed Gerry Halstead cleaning his boat.

" 'Morning, Gerry. How's the fishing?"

" 'Mornin'." Gerry removed his glove to shake Ellis's hand.

"Looks like a good catch. Is it taken?" Ellis peered into a basket crawling with lobsters.

"Not yet, you buying?"

"I'll take the lot. How much?"

"I was hoping to make ten dollars." Gerry raked his thinning brown hair.

"Ten it is." Ellis pealed off a ten-dollar bill. "Here you go."

"Wow, thanks." Gerry lifted the basket of lobsters. "You throwing a party?"

"Sure enough. Wanna come?" Ellis invited.

Gerry chuckled. "I'm afraid I wouldn't have any lobsters to bring."

"Not a problem. Bring a salad, rice and beans, or something to drink."

"All right, what time?"

"Six, my place. If you recall, I bought the Captain Curtis house."

"I'll be there. Thanks. What's the special occasion? Getting hitched to that pretty nanny?"

Ellis's cheeks burned. "No. It started as a meal for Cook's family. It's kinda grown."

"That tends to happen around here. I'll get the wife to cook up something. See you at six."

"*Adios.*" Ellis waved and headed home. The fish purchased and several more families invited, he needed to stop by the church next and get some tables and chairs. Naturally, Pastor Williams and his family would be coming. Ellis laughed and quickened his pace toward the church.

❧

"You what?" Bea couldn't believe her ears. "You've invited more?"

Ellis chuckled and pulled her into his embrace. "Shh, dear, it's going to be all right. Trust me."

A shiver slithered down her spine from Ellis's warm breath on her ear. "Ellis, we don't have food for fifty people."

"Sure we do. And other folks are bringing stuff too."

"I've never given a party like this." And never would she plan one this way either. Her mother had taught her well. Occasions of this magnitude took months of planning.

"It's the island way. Trust me." Ellis's firm hand rested on the back of her neck. His thumb slowly worked its way across her cheek. Bea's knees started to tremble. He held her steady. "Do you trust me, Bea?" he whispered in her ear.

What could she do? He exuded confidence, and in his arms she did believe him. It made no logical sense, but she did trust him to pull this party off. "We'll need to make some more. . ." she was at a loss as to what to make. "Something."

"Shh, come here, honey." Ellis led her to the parlor. "Sit down."

Ellis knelt before her. His blue-gray eyes steeled with confidence. "I've been out of proper society for a long time. But I do recall some things, and I know my mother would be in a tizzy if a party this size was suddenly thrust upon her. So I understand your fears. But darling, on the island things are done differently. You don't need to make any more food.

There's plenty coming. Pastor Williams is bringing the tables and chairs. . ."

"Pastor Williams is coming?" Bea was in shock. The house wasn't ready for a visit from the clergy. "Oh my. We need to get the house ready."

"No, we don't. Bea, look at me." He gently took her chin into his hand and nudged it so it was face-to-face with his. Bea quieted her soul and concentrated on the handsome man before her. His thumb touched her lips. "Oh, Ellis."

Ellis leaned into her and lifted slightly, kissing her forehead. Bea's eyes closed and soaked in the nearness, the soft touch of his lips upon her forehead. His whispered words brought her back to reality.

"We have an audience."

Bea's cheeks flamed. Ellis leaned away from her.

"Excuse me, Mr. Ellis, Miss Bea. Brian Fairfield is here." Cook departed after her announcement. Ellis stood up and went to the front hall. Bea could hear his conversation. "Thank you, Brian, you did great. Bring them to the kitchen for Cook."

"Yes, sir. Oh, Mom said we'd be coming, and she's fixing a few pies and the Spanish rice."

"Great. Pastor Williams will be here shortly with the tables and chairs. Do you think you can lend him a hand?"

"Certainly, Mr. Southard."

Bea clasped her hands, closed her eyes, and silently prayed. *Father, give me understanding regarding this "party," and give me strength regarding Ellis and my attraction to him.*

❧

Lord, the woman is incredible. Thank you for putting her in my path, Ellis silently prayed, walking back into the parlor. "Bea," he whispered. "I'm sorry, I shouldn't have been so forward. You were so worked up about the party I didn't know what else to do."

Her eyes fluttered open. "So, you get me flustered in another way?"

"No, the kiss was an impulse and for that I apologize."

Bea smiled. "You're forgiven."

"Good, now I want you to go to your cottage. Relax. Take a nap, perhaps, and freshen up for this evening."

She narrowed her gaze. "Mr. Southard, are you suggesting I'm not presentable?"

Ellis prayed she was teasing. "Precisely," he teased back.

Bea's mouth gaped open.

"I can tease, too, my dear." Ellis grinned. "Besides, would I have kissed you if I found you so unattractive?"

"You did miss," she coyly replied, and rose from the sofa.

"Touché." Whatever possessed him to think he could battle wits with this woman? "If you'll excuse me, beautiful, the swine needs turning."

Bea laughed and headed toward the kitchen. "Bea, your cottage is that way." Ellis pointed to the front door.

"But. . ."

"But, nothing. I want you well tonight. Now go." He smiled to tame the intensity of his order.

She mocked a salute. "Aye, Captain."

Ellis groaned inwardly. He'd done it again. Delegating—giving orders and expecting them followed—came with being the boss. Bea, however, was not his employee.

Once outside, he turned the pig, added some wood to the fire, and began raking the lawn free of debris. Folks would begin arriving in a couple of hours. Pastor Williams pulled in with his wagon loaded with tables and chairs. The fishermen delivered their fish. The house was alive with activity. Every so often he saw Bea peeking out a window. *This isn't right,* he chided himself, and dropped his rake. A few long strides and he was rounding the corner of Bea's cottage. "Bea!" he hollered.

"Ellis, don't come in!" Bea cried out.

"I won't. Forgive me. If you want to help or even be a part of greeting everyone, please come out."

"In a minute," Bea whispered behind the closed door. "Ellis, would you send Cook over please?"

"Are you all right?"

"I'm fine, I just need a woman's assistance."

Of course, a corset. Personally he'd prefer the woman to not be so tied up, but this being a social occasion, and Beatrice wanting to impress, he understood her need. "I'll fetch her. And honey, I'm sorry, I didn't mean to order you."

"I understand, Ellis, and I did need the rest, but I like being in the midst of things. It's been driving me crazy sitting in this cottage."

Ellis chuckled. "I want you in the midst of things," he mumbled.

"What? Speak up, Ellis, I can't hear you through the door."

"Never mind, I'll tell you later."

❧

Bea heard the gravel under Ellis's feet protest his weight as he walked away from her cottage. "Did he say what I think I heard, Lord?" Bea moved to her bedroom in the back of the cottage. On the bed she had laid out her lilac summer dress with a white laced collar and pearl buttons down the bodice. The skirt of the dress gathered at the waist and descended into a V shape in the front.

The door creaked open and Cook called out, "It's me, Bea, what do you need me for?"

"My corset."

Cook entered the bedroom. "The light one, I hope. Goodness, child, that is a pretty dress."

"Thank you and, yes, the light one. I want to be comfortable."

"Turn around," Cook ordered.

Bea turned. "How's it going in the kitchen?"

"All done, just been cleaning up. Gonna wash and change after I get you hooked up here." Cook groaned straining at the laces.

"Ouch, that's tight enough. I'm not that vain," Bea giggled.

"Sorry. Want me to help you slip the dress over your head?"

"Yes, thanks."

"I used a slip-knot. Just pull your right-hand string and it should unfasten. If not, holler and I'll come over."

Bea reached back and found the right-hand string Cook mentioned. Soon they had her dress slipped over her head and flowing down to the floor.

"Mercy, Child, you are beautiful. Mr. Ellis gonna have a time keeping his mind on his company and not on you." Cook grinned.

"I hope so." Bea winked.

"You know, with Pastor Williams coming over tonight, we could make this into a wedding."

"Hush. We're not ready," Bea admonished.

"Don't take much more than what I saw in the living room. Admit it child, you love him."

"Cook, I think I do, but how can you love someone so quickly?"

"It's a mystery, but some folks just get hit like that. George and I did. Once I met him, my heart was aflutter. I couldn't think of anything but George. Of course, my parents had a thing to say about that, but in the end we were married inside a year."

"A year?" Bea didn't think she could wait that long. On the other hand, a year's formal engagement period would be expected back home.

"Yes'm. 'Course, George was away most of that year. If'n he was at home, I imagine we would have been married much sooner."

Bea felt her cheeks flush.

"Truth, is all. Of course, we never told the children that until they were older, much older." Cook winked.

Bea reached out and hugged Cook. "Thank you, Francine, you're a good friend."

"I'm honored to be yours, Miss Bea." Cook patted Bea on her back. "Do you need help with your hair?"

"No thank you. Ellis likes it down, but that's not really proper, so I thought I'd put it in a French braid."

"Sounds beautiful. Well, if'n you don't need me, I best get cleaned up. I smell like fish. You wouldn't believe how much Mr. Ellis bought."

Bea closed her eyes and let out a small sigh. "No, I'm sure I wouldn't."

Cook departed and Bea sat down at her vanity. She took down her tight bun and began combing out her hundred strokes.

A sudden knock and crash at her front door startled her.

eighteen

"Nanna!" Richard cried with excitement.

"Richard, you frightened me." Bea placed her brush down on the vanity.

"Sorry." Richard jumped up on her bed and bounced. "I'm so excited. Uncle Ellis said everybody is coming."

Bea chuckled. "I can see you're excited. What have you been doing? You're filthy."

"Helping."

"Helping with what, dirt?"

"No, silly, raking the leaves and broken trees and stuff."

"Oh." Bea smiled. "I'm sure you've been a big help."

"Uncle Ellis said I needed to get washed up."

Oh dear, Bea had forgotten about getting Richard ready first. Dirt would attach to this dress like a moth to a light. "Can you wash up by yourself?"

Richie nodded his head.

"You wash up, and I'll help you put on your Sunday clothes."

"Can I play in them?"

"Of course not," Bea lightly scolded. "You know that."

"I wanna play the games with the other kids. Can I wear something else?"

Naturally he would want to play.

"Of course." Bea wondered if she had made the wrong choice in her dress.

"Richard," Ellis called from outside Bea's door. "I told you to go clean up."

"Nanna always helps me," Richard called back.

When Richie came barreling in, Bea had completed twenty brush strokes on her hair. "Ellis, you may come in."

The door creaked open. "Richard, go to the house, Son. "I. . .I'll. . . Bea, you're beautiful," Ellis proclaimed.

"Thank you. Richie, you go on. I'll be right up there to help you pick out your clothes," Bea encouraged.

"I can do it, if I can wear play clothes."

The boy was growing up, Bea thought with a smile. "All right."

Richard slipped off the bed, leaving a streak of dirt behind him. "I'll see you at the big house, Uncle Ellis."

Ellis stood there motionless, speechless. "Please stand up," he finally spoke.

Bea trembled and stood. "Do you approve?"

"Goodness, do you have to ask? I've never seen anyone as beautiful."

Heat fused with joy and painted a faint blush on her cheeks. "Thank you."

The intensity of his attraction forced her to restrain an urge to jump into his arms. She needed to break the tension between them. "You're a handsome man, Ellis Southard, but I've seen you look much better." She winked.

❧

Ellis looked at his blackened hands. Amused by her ability to understate the obvious, he smiled. "I'm in need of a good scrubbing."

"At the very least."

"I. . .I need to go. If I don't, I'll soil that dress." A desire to wrap her in his arms fought to have its way. Ellis thought of the Lord and how He would behave given this situation, and swallowed hard, silently thanking God for His grace.

Bea giggled. "You do and you'll not hear the end of it."

"Later, my love." Ellis wiggled his reddish brown eyebrows

and turned to leave.

A faint whisper tickled his ears. "I'm looking forward to it."

"I heard that, Beatrice Smith. You're a siren for certain, here to test me."

His hand reached the latch of her front door.

"Or vice versa," she replied.

He didn't have time for this playful banter, although he fought a tremendous desire to continue it. As if working his way through a thick marsh, he pushed himself toward the house. Guests would be arriving shortly.

Mounting the stairs two at a time, he arrived at his room in short order. He grimaced at the sight of his filthy face in the mirror. Sweat mingled with black soil and small bits of decaying leaves plastered his face and beard. Looking at the amount of dirt in his hair and on his body, Ellis slipped on a robe and headed for the outside shower, an ingenious contraption of a fifty-gallon barrel with a spigot. When one pulled on the string attached to the spigot, water sprayed down on him.

❧

Showered and dressed, Ellis entered the parlor. Bea stood at the far wall examining a hand-painted vase from the Far East. "Am I more presentable now, Miss Smith?"

Bea turned with the grace of a dove floating on the wind. Scanning him from head to toe, she spoke. "Mr. Southard, you are most handsome indeed."

Ellis stepped further into the room. "Come here, love."

Bea placed the vase back on the shelf and walked toward him with elegant poise.

"Your hair, it's beautiful. What style is this?"

"It's a French braid. I know you like my hair worn down, yet a woman should always wear it up. So this braid allows it to be tied neatly in the back."

"Bea, you're incredible. . ." Ellis reached for her delicate fingers. She slipped her hands into his. "I. . ."

"Uncle Ellis!" Richard yelled. "They're here."

"Later, my love," Ellis whispered in her ear. Then he took in a deep breath and released her.

He turned toward the doorway and marched to the front door. Pulling it open, he greeted everyone. "Welcome, come on in." Members of Cook's family started pouring in. As the door was about to close, another group, and then another entered as well. The house was soon brimming with people.

Ellis encouraged the men to join him outside at the pit. The ladies began carrying out the food to the tables in the backyard. The children followed Richard as he first showed them his room, then the various nooks and crannies of the house.

Bea mingled well, Ellis noted. She spoke with loving grace. Constantly throughout the evening he watched her. Occasionally, he would catch her watching him. All different ages and races mingled together, the house and yard overflowing with people.

Key West is a good place to raise a child, Ellis decided. *But what about the homestead—my brother's wishes? I must make a decision regarding that property someday,* he mused. *But today is not that day.*

Pastor Williams, in his black and white preacher's suit, walked up to him with a hand outstretched. "Quite a feast, Ellis. Thank you for inviting us."

"My pleasure, Pastor. Thank you for the use of the tables and chairs."

"They're always available. So, tell me about this Miss Smith. . .will she be staying on?"

"That's hard to say, Pastor." How could he admit his feelings for Bea when they hadn't yet discussed them?

"Does she have a commitment back north?" Pastor Williams inquired, searching Ellis for an answer.

"No, but I can't ask her to stay on as the child's nanny."

Pastor Williams lowered his voice. "Why not?"

Ellis looked at Bea. Pastor Williams caught his glance. "I see." Pastor Williams smiled. "If you don't mind me making a suggestion, totally unasked for, I wouldn't let that one slip from my hands, if I were you." Pastor Williams slapped Ellis on the back. "God's blessings, Son. You're going to need it."

Ellis swore he heard the pastor chuckling under his breath as he walked away. Was it that obvious? Heat blazed on his high cheekbones.

" 'Evening, Ellis." Marc Dabny sidled up beside him, his swollen belly lined with a gold chain. "Quite a crowd here tonight. Anything special going on?"

"Just invited a few friends, and it kinda grew." Ellis smiled, grateful for the distraction.

Marc whistled for Lizzy, Cook's daughter, as she walked past. "Hey, get me a drink."

Lizzy turned to face Marc, but held her tongue.

"She's a guest, Marc. You can get your own drink, like everyone else here." Ellis held back his emotions.

"Excuse me?" Marc confronted Ellis face-to-face. "I can understand you throwing a party for your workers, but to consider them guests. . . Are you daft?"

"Forgive my friend, Lizzy. He seems to have forgotten his manners." Ellis stood toe-to-toe with Marc, towering over the balding man. "Lizzy is my guest. Her mother works for me, but she is not my employee. May I suggest you apologize?"

"You're daft, I'm not apologizing to no n. . ."

Ellis grabbed Marc by the collar and lifted him to his toes. "Not in my house. No one, not anyone, uses that word in my house. Do you understand, Marc?"

Marc's bulging eyes blazed with anger as he nodded his assent.

Ellis eased him back to the ground. "I believe our business

partnership will not be pursued, Mr. Dabny."

"You'd throw away a solid offer for the likes. . ."

Ellis knitted his eyebrows.

". . .for. . ."

Ellis leaned closer and set his jaw.

"those. . .those. . .people?" Marc spat on the ground.

"Any day. I believe you've worn out your welcome, Mr. Dabny. Have a good evening." Ellis turned his back to Marc and stepped back into the crowd which had gathered behind him.

Marc spat at Ellis's feet. "You're a fool, Ellis Southard, an absolute fool."

Ellis refused to bait the man, but simply ignored him and walked up to Lizzy. "My apologies, Lizzy." He reached for her hand and bowed. "You're welcome in my home anytime."

Bea watched as Lizzy's eyes pooled with tears. Bea's own eyes threatened to stream. She bit the inside of her cheek to hold back the tears. Ellis had handled Marc with absolute authority. She was so proud of him. By the looks of the folks gathered around him, they were proud of him as well.

❧

Bea worked her way to one of the tables. On its far corner a lantern glowed. She sat down and waited. She'd been on her feet all evening greeting folks, learning people's names, and their relationship to Ellis. She rubbed the back of her calves. She hadn't been in high heels since she arrived, apart from the short outing to church the other day.

"Care if I sit down?" Mrs. Williams, the pastor's wife, asked, holding a bald baby with a toothless grin.

"Of course not." Bea placed her hands in front of her on the table.

"Are your feet hurting?"

"I'm afraid so. I haven't been in high heels much."

"Hardly wear them myself. Can't go chasing eight children in high heels." Mrs. Williams bounced the little one on her lap.

"I can't imagine. Chasing one child keeps me busy."

Mrs. Williams chuckled.

"Will you be staying, Beatrice?"

Bea didn't know what to say. To respond that she had fallen madly in love with Ellis and prayed she would be staying at his side forever was not an option. "I'm waiting on a ship bound for New York."

"So, Mr. Southard doesn't want to hire you on as Richard's nanny? Or do you have obligations back home?"

"Truth be told, I have no obligations. But Mr. Southard doesn't believe he can hire me to stay on as Richard's nanny."

Mrs. Williams's pleasant face contorted with confusion.

"It's complicated."

Mrs. Williams's brown eyes softened. "I'm sorry, I didn't mean to pry."

"It's hard to explain. Ellis—I mean Mr. Southard—learned of my social status and he feels it is improper for me to continue on, especially since he is quite capable of hiring someone."

"That doesn't sound like the man who just. . ." Mrs. Williams caught herself and stopped. "I'm sorry, I have a tendency to rattle off my thoughts before thinking them through."

"Mrs. Williams. . ."

"Edith, please."

"All right. Edith. Please don't think poorly of Mr. Southard. In our community back home I already created quite a scandal by staying on as Richard's nanny. But over time, many came to realize I deeply loved Richard's mother and would honor my commitment to her."

"There seems to be a lot in that pretty head of yours, dear.

Is it your prayer to stay with Richard?"

Bea placed her hands in her lap.

Edith's black hair sparkled from the light—or was it tears threading her eyelids? Bea wasn't certain. The baby cooed at a moth flying around the lantern.

Edith reached her hand and placed it upon Bea's. "The Lord will give you the desires of your heart. Trust Him."

Bea nodded her head, afraid to speak. The desires of her heart had shifted drastically since the day she first arrived on the island. No longer did she simply want to not separate from Richard. Now, she no longer wanted to part from the man who had captured her heart.

She glanced up and saw Ellis saying good night to a few families with younger children. He lifted a small child and tossed him in the air. *He's so good with children, Lord.*

"There's something more than your social status keeping you from being Richard's nanny," Edith whispered.

Bea nodded. She couldn't deny it any longer. Of course Cook knew, but was Ellis ready to have the town, the pastor and his wife, know of their budding relationship? "Please don't think poorly of Ellis, Mrs. . . .I mean, Edith. Cook has moved into the house, and I am remaining in the cottage."

"I do not thinking badly of you or Ellis. Go with your heart, dear. Trust God to work out the details."

"Thank you."

"Forgive me for leaving so, but I'll never get these children to bed if I don't start rounding them up now." Edith smiled. "Good night, Beatrice. It's a pleasure meeting you. I'll be praying."

Bea started to get up.

"No dear, sit. . .relax. You've done enough."

"Good night, Edith, and thank you."

"You're welcome. Stop by the parsonage anytime if you

would need to talk or just want to visit." Edith slipped back into the darkness, calling her children.

A parade of lanterns exited Ellis's home and worked their way down the street. *What a truly different place this is, Lord,* she pondered.

❧

Ellis said good-bye to Pastor Williams and his family. Some of Cook's family members were helping with the cleanup. Most folks were gone, and Bea sat alone at a table. He longed to be next to her. But one person after another kept them apart.

Ellis looked to the right and left. No one. He grinned and hurried over to Bea's table. "Finally, we can be together." He sat down beside her. Tears edged her eyelids. "Bea, have you been crying?"

She smiled and shook her head, no.

Ellis brushed his thumb up to her eye. A tiny droplet of water sat on his thumb. "Then what's this?"

"I've been holding them back," she whispered.

"What's the matter?"

"Nothing."

"Nothing?" Do women cry at nothing? He thought back to his mother. There were a few times when he found her with tears in her eyes.

Ellis scooted closer on the wooden bench and leaned toward her ear. "I've longed to be this close to you all night."

"Oh, Ellis." Bea reached her arms around his shoulders.

Ellis completed their embrace, pulling her closer.

"I'm so proud of you, the way you stood up to Mr. Dabny tonight."

Ellis squeezed her gently. "Thank you. The man is a. . . I won't say it."

Bea giggled. "I think I know what you were going to say."

"Hmm, you're dangerous, do you know that?"

"Me, dangerous?" She pulled back and looked him straight in the eye. "You sir, with your gallant behavior. . . And tonight—this entire evening—I can't believe you pulled it off with no planning. It was just like you said it would be. Folks brought plenty of food. Everyone enjoyed themselves. I'm amazed, Mr. Southard, truly amazed."

"Amazed enough to. . ." Ellis trailed her lips with his thumb.

Bea's eyes closed in anticipation.

Did he dare? If he kissed her there would be no turning back. He wouldn't be able to let her leave. Everything shouted she was the one for him. His soulmate, his gift from God. But for so long he had given up on the possibility of having a wife, a woman who could love him, accept him, forgive him.

But how could he resist her? No, he would not resist. "I love you, Bea," he whispered before her velvet lips touched his.

She kissed him back. He tightened his hold of her. She tightened her hold on him.

Time dissolved into a blanket of tranquillity. Slowly he pulled away. He opened his eyes. A blush, the shade of a pale pink rose, accented her delicate nose.

Bea's eyes fluttered open. They were wide with passion and honesty. "I love you, Ellis." Her fingers trailed his swollen lips.

Ellis felt a tug on his pant leg. "Uncle Ellis, are you and Nanna married now?"

Ellis groaned.

Bea coughed out, "No."

"But uncle Ellis said that when you kissed you were married!" Richard whined.

"Richard, I said after the pastor says the man and woman

are married they can kiss."

"And you were kissing."

"Honey, your uncle Ellis and I were kissing, but we aren't married. We like each other," Bea pleaded. *How do you make a four year old understand?* she wondered.

"But. . .," Richard pouted, "don't you have to marry Nanna now?"

Ellis left her side and squatted next to Richard. "Son, a man has to ask a woman first if she would like to be his wife."

"Did you ask her?" Richard held his mouth firm.

"No, Son."

"Are you gonna?" Richard folded his arms over his chest.

"I'm thinking about it." Ellis squirmed.

Bea smiled. Was he really? She'd been thinking about it forever, or so it seemed. And yet it had only been a little over a week.

"Then ask her."

"Richie. . . ," Bea admonished. She hoped Ellis wouldn't think she put Richard up to such nonsense.

"I might just do that, Son." Ellis turned to Bea.

"Ellis, you don't have to do this." Bea squirmed on the bench. Was he really going to ask her? Now? Here? In Richard's presence?

Ellis smiled a wicked grin and took her by the hand. "If I ask you, Bea, it's because I want to do this, not because of Richard's pleading."

"Oh, my!" Bea needed a cool cloth, her cheeks were on fire.

"Beatrice Smith, you are the most incredible woman I've ever known. First, you've raised my nephew through all sorts of perils, and all because of a love for a friend. Second, you showed me how to release myself from my past and to allow God's forgiveness in my life. Third, you're profoundly beautiful inside and out, and I would deeply be honored if you would consent to become my wife."

Bea trembled. Her hands shook as they nested inside of Ellis's larger ones and she noticed his were trembling too.

"Are you married now?" Richard said impatiently.

"No, Son. You have to let the woman answer first."

"Oh. Answer, Nanna."

Bea chuckled. This had to be a first, being coached by a four year old for a proposal of marriage. "I'm going to answer your uncle Ellis."

"When?" Richard placed his hands on his hips and tapped his foot.

Ellis bit his lips. Bea did the same and composed herself. "As soon as someone stops interrupting me."

"Me?" Richard asked.

Bea nodded. "Yes, you. Now hush for a minute."

"Ellis, I love you with all my heart and soul, and I would be truly honored to be your wife."

"Is that a 'yes'?" Richard asked.

Bea and Ellis roared in laughter. Ellis composed himself first. "Yes, Son, that was a yes."

"Yippee! Nanna has married uncle Ellis!" Richie ran into the house screaming.

"Are you certain, Ellis?"

Ellis climbed up off the ground, brushing the sand off his pant knee. He sat down beside her on the bench again. "Quite, my love." He reached his arm across her shoulders. "I wasn't going to ask you so soon, or with an audience, but I was going to ask."

Bea combed his beard with her fingers. Soft warmth coiled around her fingertips.

"Would you be needing a year's engagement period before we marry?" Ellis asked.

"Not if I can help it," Bea blurted out.

"Good, I was hoping you wouldn't want to wait. How's next week?"

Bea chuckled. "Too soon. Although Cook said we'd be married by the end of next week."

"I always did like Cook." Ellis nuzzled into her neck.

"Ellis, could we wait until my parents can come, or reply if they can't?"

"Of course. I don't want to wait forever, but I'll wait as long as it takes."

Bea wrapped her arms around his neck and gave him a quick kiss.

"Now you two better stop that. Unless what the boy said is true and you're already married," Cook chuckled.

"Oh dear." Bea blushed. "He said that?"

"Yup, the entire house knows you were kissin' and are married."

Bea groaned.

"Well he got part of it right. We're getting married, Cook. Bea's honored me by saying she'd be my wife."

"Well, praise the Good Lord in heaven. It's about time the two of you got it straight."

Bea and Ellis chuckled.

"Suppose we ought to go in the house and correct the rumors our son has been spreading?" Ellis asked.

"Our son," she whispered. *Our son.* Richard would finally be her son.

"Yes, our son." Ellis squeezed her gently.

"I suppose so." Bea hated the thought of being out of Ellis's arms. Perhaps her parents would understand if she were to just write them and tell them her happy news.

No, she reasoned. They'd be fit to be tied. She and Ellis would have to wait. And waiting wouldn't be such a bad thing. They still needed to get to know one another better.

Ellis stood and held his hand out for her to grasp. He curled her arm into the crook of his elbow and he led her to the house. "Come on, Cook, they're your family. Help us straighten this mess out."

Cook chuckled. "You has got yourselves into this mess, you can get yourselves out. I'm goin' to enjoy watching ya."

epilogue

Three months later

"Mom, help me?" Bea pleaded. "I'm so nervous I can't clasp this pearl necklace."

"Relax, Bea." Joanna Smith eased the necklace from her daughter's hands.

"I can't believe my wedding day is finally here." Bea looked at the high-collared, French-laced wedding gown that she, her mother, Cook, and Lizzy had sewn. Every day and evening for the past month, they had worked on the gown, the train, the headpiece, Lizzy's gown, Cook's dress and her mom's dress. Bea often thought Ellis had it easy. He simply went into town and hired a tailor.

She put her hair in a French braid, interwoven with pearls.

Joanna's eyes teared. "You're so beautiful, Bea."

"Thanks, Mom. I hope Ellis is pleased."

Lizzy laughed. "The man would have to be dead not to notice how beautiful you are." Bea smiled at the woman who had quickly become her closest friend.

"Thank you, Lizzy."

Although Lizzy still mourned her husband's death, she was free from the anger toward the white man who had killed him. Prejudice still existed in the world, even on Key West, but Bea and Lizzy learned the only way to battle it was one person at a time. And to hate an entire race because of the actions of others was foolishness to God.

A gentle knock on the door caused Bea to stiffen.

Her mother opened the door and smiled. "You're looking mighty handsome today, dear."

Bea watched her father enter the room, his sideburns laced with gray, his mustache completely gray, and his receding hairline glowing with maturity. His eyes sparkled. "You're beautiful, Beatrice. Almost as pretty as your mother."

"Thanks, Daddy."

"Are you ready?"

"Yes." Bea stepped forward and captured her father's elbow. It was firm and comforting. Today she needed his confidence.

"Thank you for coming, Dad."

"I wouldn't have missed this for the world. Come on, Precious, let's go meet your groom."

Bea took in a deep breath and stepped to the edge of the doorway.

The music began. Ellis stepped out with Pastor Williams and Richard. Richard looked so handsome in his junior-sized black tails with a white shirt and black bow tie. Beatrice didn't know he had Richard fitted; it was one of many surprises he had planned for her today.

Ellis watched as Lizzy came down the aisle, followed by Ruth Williams, Pastor Williams four-year-old daughter. She tossed the flower petals in front of her with precision, stopping to make certain the area was properly covered before moving on. Ellis grinned and spied Pastor Williams enjoying his daughter's performance.

The music shifted and the congregation stood. Ellis watched as Bea's father rounded the corner and a billow of white followed. His heart raced, his palms instantly dampened. "Oh Lord, she's beautiful," he whispered.

Richard tugged on Ellis's pant leg. "Nanna's pretty."

Ellis smiled. "Yes, she is."

It had taken a while, but Richard finally understood that marriage was more than kissing and holding hands, that it was a pledge between a man and a woman with God and others watching.

Bea was so close he wanted to reach out and take her hand.

Instead, Ellis held himself back and waited for the pastor's cue.

"And who gives this woman to be married to this man?"

"Her mother and I do," Jamison Smith answered in a strained voice.

Ellis reached out his hand to his bride. Jamison slipped her hand into his. Ellis's strong hand encircled hers. They turned and faced Pastor Williams.

"Dearly beloved. . ." Pastor Williams continued with the service. When he reached the pronouncement that they were husband and wife, he proclaimed, "You may now kiss the bride."

Ellis lifted her veil and cherished the sweet kiss of his new wife, then felt the all too familiar tug on his pant leg. "Are we married now?" Richard asked.

Bea and Ellis started to bubble with giggles. Soon the entire congregation was laughing.

"Yes, Richie, Bea and I are married," Ellis replied.

"Yippee!" Richard screamed, then cupped his mouth with his hands. "I'm sorry." He stood up straight and placed his hands by his side.

Bea smiled. "It's okay, Son. We're a family now; you can relax."

Bea embraced her new husband and was reminded of Ecclesiastes 3:5 once again. Her time of embracing had come. She held Ellis even tighter.

A Letter To Our Readers

Dear Reader:

In order that we might better contribute to your reading enjoyment, we would appreciate your taking a few minutes to respond to the following questions. We welcome your comments and read each form and letter we receive. When completed, please return to the following:

Rebecca Germany, Fiction Editor
Heartsong Presents
PO Box 719
Uhrichsville, Ohio 44683

1. Did you enjoy reading *A Time to Embrace?*
   - ❑ Very much. I would like to see more books by this author!
   - ❑ Moderately
     I would have enjoyed it more if ____________________

     ____

     ____

2. Are you a member of **Heartsong Presents**? Yes ❑ No ❑
   If no, where did you purchase this book?____________

   ____

3. How would you rate, on a scale from 1 (poor) to 5 (superior), the cover design?____________________

4. On a scale from 1 (poor) to 10 (superior), please rate the following elements.

   _____ Heroine   _____ Plot

   _____ Hero   _____ Inspirational theme

   _____ Setting   _____ Secondary characters

5. These characters were special because______________________

____

____

6. How has this book inspired your life?______________________

____

____

7. What settings would you like to see covered in future **Heartsong Presents** books?______________________

____

____

8. What are some inspirational themes you would like to see treated in future books?______________________

____

____

9. Would you be interested in reading other **Heartsong Presents** titles? Yes ❑ No ❑

10. Please check your age range:

❑ Under 18 ❑ 18-24 ❑ 25-34
❑ 35-45 ❑ 46-55 ❑ Over 55

11. How many hours per week do you read?______________________

Name ____

Occupation ____

Address ____

City ______________ State __________ Zip __________